Robotic Humamoids Book 2.

Steve Evans

Published by Steve Evans, 2024.

ROBOTIC HUMAMOIDS BOOK 2.

First edition. November 3, 2024.

ISBN: 979-8227726810

Written by Steve Evans.

Table of Contents

Robotic Humanoids.
Book 2.

The human Micro Quantum Brain.

By

Steve Evans

Introduction.

It had been sometime since us humans had evacuated from the old world and made that long and eventual journey in that huge spacecraft hotel to permanently accommodate the new planet our Humanoid Robots had found for us way back in 2026. *(As in the original story (Robotic Humanoids Book 1.)* Some of us did miss the old world, but not on our new planet our living environment and social and business life was proving to be superior to what could ever had been achieved in the old world, and we were able and competent knowing that as we and our children through the personal use of Artificial Intelligence we would mentally evolve and become superior mentally intelligent human beings.

I had been fortunate, I was only two years old when I was evacuated to this lovely new planet of ours, and although I never really knew Vanessa, I occasionally saw her and met her through our school years. My name is Daniel (Dan) and just a couple of years ago I was working on a Quantum Timing project when I met the now elderly Professor Salman, Vanessa's father, he was impressed with my work and invited me to visit his home to talk about our mutual project, robotic quantum physics incorporating Artificial Intelligence (AI).

It was there that I met Vanessa, now a beautifully grown young woman, we talked, we laughed and remembered the years when we were so young and learning so much from our parents and teachers influence.

We were just finishing our meal when Vanessa's mum suddenly said. "What you are laughing about, talk about something more important than your childhood."

Vanessa put down her knife and fork, looked at her mum and said.

"Mum, don't be so rude, you know we have a lot to catch up on. So don't worry you don't have to listen to what we are saying."

Vanessa's dad intervened. "Leave them alone, their getting on fine, let's take our coffee into to the lounge and leave them to it."

And here we are a year later, married and trying for our first baby.

The humanoid robots with very active helping and working with the administration and development of this new world. And continued to learn to cooperate and work with us in helping to create our new world, 'Eunaton' they wanted to become more human and learn to be more like us, and the more they learnt about us the more they became to be like us. They began to understand how we humans operate, how we think and live and the way we activate our thinking powers.

They learnt how we thought and the need to express our feelings, allowing our thoughts to determine our physical actions. And that is the doing process and we act from our ability to use the creative process of the human thinking power. And the process and implementation of Artificial Intelligence began to take precedence within the minds of our computer programmers.

And the humanoids quickly learnt that our human consciousness had evolved and created and separated us from the basic animal environment. And had to accept that they were just Artificial Intelligent Machines needing to re-charge from convenient power sources and occasional supplementary charging from the sun and daylight.

Chapter 1.
A human mental humanoid experiment.

Vanessa's baby was born in September 2037 and her father Dan was over the moon, they had a son, and he wanted to name him 'Quinten'. Vanessa agreed and thought what a lovely name it was for their son. In Quentin's infant years, he quickly learnt to talk, read, and continually asked many questions about the robotic helpers, why were they different and so clever. Both Vanessa and Dan realised he had above average intellect and was relating more to his robotic tutor than to his other childhood activities. And has he grew out of his infant stage it was obvious that he was developing a mental awareness of the robotic humanoid superior intelligence and his preference for their intellectual company.

They decided to talk to the Professor about their concern regarding Quentin exceptional and unfamiliar behaviour.

Professor Salam, James and Quanto were pleased to meet Dan and Vanessa in their office and were more than interested in the above average intellect and activity of young Quentin's intellect.

The Professor said. "It seems that he wants to think and act like his robotic tutor and is wanting to know how to relate to them on an equal basis."

"Yes, said James. It appears that his thoughts are above the mental ability of your feelings and thoughts, and if that is the case, then we are dealing with quiet complex and an unusual problem."

"We know that, answered Dan. That's why we're here, we need to know how best to deal with his future education?"

"First, said the Professor's. Get him to come to see us, on his own. We would like to ask him a few questions and get him to talk to us."

"Okay, that's a good idea. Said Dan. We'll ask him and give you a call."

James intervened and said. "And we could introduce him to Quanto, our humanoid assistant.."

Vanessa said. "He would love that." As Dan nodded in agreement.

Quinton got quite excited about meeting the Professor and their robot Quanto. As he entered the professor's office, he immediately noticed the robotic figure standing by the window obviously charging its system from the bright daylight. The Professor sitting in the usual place behind his desk with James sitting to one side, as James stood up, he gestured Quinton to sit down and said.

"Hi Quinton, gesturing to the Professor he continued, this is Professor Salman. And looking over to the window said. "This is our robotic assistant 'Quanto' who we understand you would like to meet."

"Yes, I have been studying artificial intelligence (AI) on my computer, and I want to experience direct contact with a new quantum robot."

"Well here, you will have the opportunity, first we need to ask some questions."

"I know, Quinton said. You need to check that I have the mental ability to work with your quantum robot."

"Good, said the Professor. James set up the IQ test for Quinton and let's get started."

The average intelligence quotient (IQ) is between 85 and 115. But this number can vary between countries, states, and even geographical regions. IQ stands for "intelligence quotient" and is a standard of measurement used to assess a person's mental aptitude compared to a group of their peers.

They find out that Quinton's IQ is 130.

The Professor showed his surprise, nodding his head he said.

"It looks like young Quinton, that you definitely have a superior intelligence, and you'll be quite capable of conversing with our robot assistant."

Quinton showed his excitement. "Can I talk to it now?"

"Yes of course."

"James, wake-up Quanto and let Quinton introduce himself."

Quanto turned and said. *"Hello, how can I help."*

Quinton gulped, took a deep breath, and said breathlessly.

"My name is Quinton, and I have a very important question for you."

"I will do my best, what is your question?"

"Is it possible for the human brain to access an artificial intelligent microchip and internally program and create an algorithm."

"Yes, it is possible. Give me a moment and I will answer your question in detail."

The Professor and James were quite surprised at Quintin's obvious knowledge of artificial intelligence and said.

"Looks like we have a candidate who can and will work with Quanto."

Quanto's eyes lit up, its voice came over loud and clear. *"Your scientists have already discovered a microchip that works and can control your brain's synapses activity. It is rather big and cumbersome and requires neurosurgeons' operation to insert and maintains, we know that we can reproduce a superior chip that will operate naturally through your brain's synapsis activity, and it will be small enough to be injected into the frontal lobe of your human brain. We've noticed that you've already discovered and developed a microchip that works through the control of your brain's synapsis activity. And I repeat It is big and cumbersome and requires neurosurgeons' operation to insert and maintain, we can reproduce chip that will operate the same as in your brain through the activities of your synapsis and it will be small enough to be injected into your human brain."*

Quinton looking at Professor, gesticulated with open hands and said.

"I suspected that, I felt it was possible for our brain to be able to emulate the advanced digital power of our humanoid robots."

James showing his excitement, said. "Quinton, you've already set up a good communication relationship with Quanto, your now into the future development of human artificial intelligence."

"Yes, said the Professor. And you could be our first experimental candidate."

Quinton wrinkled his face and with a wry grin said.

"Do you really think it's possible for me to be able to think like a humanoid robot?"

"We do, said James. But we need to talk to your parents first, they have to understand how the process will change your mental facilities."

"Oh, they will be okay because they know how I study the humanoid AI brainpower."

Back home is mum immediately asked.

"How did you get on with the Professor?"

"Okay, I talked to their Quanto assistant, and it confirmed what I always thought, that we can be trained to a assimilate the mental power of our humanoid robotic assistants."

"So that's why, they want to see us." Said his dad.

"Yes, I'll come with you as well?"

"No, we'd rather you'd not come, you know too much, and you would interfere with the questioning."

Quinton laughed. "Yes, I properly would, Dad. I understand their robot more than they do."

They left to meet the Professor, leaving Quinton as usual busy on his computer, studying the latest Artificial Intelligent reports.

On arrival the Professor and James are pleased to meet them again, and as they sat down the Professor said.

"You have a very intelligent young man with Quinton, and he will continue to develop his mental capabilities way above average for his age."

James intervened and said. "And we want you to understand that he could be on the threshold of becoming mentally capable of equally communicating with our advanced robotic assistants."

Vanessa, raises eyebrows saying, "We both been aware that Quinton could become quite frustrated, and we do know that we've somehow got to be able to help him and possibly control as ambitions."

"No, said James. You don't need to control him at all, he is a very capable young man, and he knows exactly what he wants to do. The problem is that we need your permission to give him the mental facilities it so desires."

"But said Dan. If you do how will he change, will he be just more mentally efficient?"

"As I've already said, he is quite capable to converse with our robotic assistants, but his brainpower is nowhere near the power of our robots, so we can now with a small injection give him the power that he so craves for."

Vanessa looked down placing her hands on her lap and said, with a worried expression. "But how would we be able to cope with Quinton, if he is thinking all just like your robots?"

The Professor slowly nodding his head. Said. "I understand, but the question here is to let him find his own way in his own time and not achieve much more than a normal artificial intelligent student would. Or we could create a situation, a mental situation with Quinton, who will be the ideal human resource to receive humanoid mental facilities."

Both Vanessa and Dan just looked at each other, the complicity of the present conversation was beyond her comprehension. Dan reached over and grasped Vanessa's shoulders, looking at her intently, he said.

"Do you want Quinton to be special, because, in view of what is just being discussed, his mental powers will be above average... so it is really down to us whether he's given the opportunity."

Vanessa paused for a moment and then said. "Then, you decide. I'm not sure how he would behave or even act if he could think like the robotic humanoids. Standing up she continued and said. Thank you both for your interest, but we need to go home now and talk to Quinton. We'll give you a call later."

As they left, the Professor said." Understandably she's a bit concerned about her son's future. But I think his dad realises his potential future."

Back home, Quinton discussed the mental micro-installation with his mum and dad and got excited when his dad said.

"Okay Quinton, I'll talk to a colleague of mine, and then will make a decision."

The Professor got a call later that day from Dan.

"Thank you both for your help, I've spoken to a colleague who also studies and produces artificial intelligent theology. He agrees, he thinks it's the best thing that could happen to Quinton."

"Good, I'm glad you took additional advice.", Said the Professor.

Then added. "I presume we can go ahead?"

"Yes, I'll get Quinton to call you".

Chapter 2.
The first human Humanoid Micro transplant.

Quinton called and said excitedly. "James, it's okay mum and dad agree, can I see you today?"

"No, arrange for your parents to call, we need to talk to them about how we intend to change your mental powers."

"Do they have to know; can't I just have it done?"

"Your parents need to understand, how the changes in your mental facilities are going to influence and reflect in your relationship with them."

"Well, couldn't I tell them?"

"No because until we have a meeting with you and your parents you will not know or understand the process involved."

"Okay, I'll asked dad to call you, when he gets home tonight."

"Good, we'll probably see you tomorrow then."

"I hope so, in the meantime I'm going to get the current AI report."

Sitting round the professors' desk both Dan and Vanessa showed their anxiety as Dan said.

"As you said when I phoned you earlier, Quinton, wants to communicate with the quantum robots but you need to talk to us first. We also want to know how it's going to change his mental facilities."

"Yes, said the Professor's. That is the leading question, he will over time become more mentally efficient than any leading scientists in the world."

Vanessa immediately sat up straight and looked at the Professor and said.

"So what would be the advantage, for Quinton and for us as well?"

"He would be the first human to have the quantum mental power of our working AI humanoid robots."

"But he will still have his human mind, his consciousness and thinking as a normal human?"

"Of course. Said the Professor. He will, but with his new mental facilities he will be a leading expert on Artificial Intelligence."

Dan turned to Quinton, who had been sitting quietly taking in the conversation, said. "That sounds what you been trying to achieve with your computer studies over the last few months."

Quinton shrugged his shoulders, raised his head, and said with conviction. "I have already asked the Professor's robotic assistant 'Quanto' if that was possible, that is what I expected and wanted to hear, especially as it is just a simple microchip injection."

The looked straight at the Professor." What was the question, and what's that about a simple injection?"

James clicked on his computer and said. "We have a recording of Quanto's answer to the question, would you like to hear it?"

Both Vanessa and Dan nodded their heads. Vanessa said. Yes, we would, can we hear it now?"

The Professor nodding his head, gesticulated to James, and said. "Yes, let them hear 'Quanto's answer."

A recording of Quanto's metallic voice came over loud and clear. Repeating the answer to Quinton's question.

"Your scientists have already discovered a microchip that works and can control your brain's synapses activity. It is big and cumbersome and requires neurosurgeons' operation to insert and maintains, we have located a superior chip that will operate naturally through your brain's synapsis activity, and it will be small enough to be injected into the frontal lobe of your human brain. The microchip that you've already discovered and developed will be superseded by the microchip injection referred to above and has already been produced in a German lab in the old world."

Dan sat there, his head bowed, looking pensive, contemplating what he had just heard. "So, he'll have to have a brain operation?"

"No, the microchip when available will be injected into the frontal lobe of his brain. An instant and normal medical injection."

"No surgery needed, added James. And no discomfort to our mentally acceptable patients."

"So, you have concluded that Quinton is an acceptable applicant?

"

"Yes, Quinton is a capable teenage mental patient ideally suitable to receive the micro insertion."

Dan looked at Vanessa, she shrugged her shoulders and said. "It's up to you Dan, you decide."

"Okay Quinton, let's get you injected."

"Oh' dad, Thanks, I'll do my best to take advantage of your decision."

A few days later, Dan got a call from the professor's office.

Hi, the medical microchip package and arrived from the German laboratory in the old world and we would like Quinton to come in and prepare for the injection.

Dan called back and said. "Can we come together; we'd like to see how it's actually done."

The Professor's office replied instantly. "Of course, this is a very important time in the history of artificial intelligence and robotic humanoids, it will be recorded, researched used and implemented probably all over the world within a few months."

Quinton, showing his usual excitement regarding artificial intelligent situations. "Wow' Dad I'm gonna be famous."

"That's up to you, you will be in a unique position., I would suggest that you initially keep a low profile, and let things develop within your new mental environment. After you have received the micro insertion, you will be the first human with a humanoid A I brain."

As they drove to the Professor's office, Quinton was on his mobile phone texting his student mates and his dad said.

"Quinton, do you realise that after you've had the microchip insertion you will mentally develop a thinking ability beyond our comprehension."

"Yes dad, I do, and I hope the Professor and James will initially help me to understand and control my thinking as it changes."

"Well, here we are, Vanessa said. We can tell the professor now to prepare for your mental operation."

As they entered the professor's office, James stood up and welcomed them in saying. "Do we have a decision today."

"Yes. So, we have to decide and allow him to have the micro insertion as you feel that Quinton is capable of accepting and assimilating the brainpower that will gradually evolve over the years."

"Yes, Quinton's brain will have the facility to develop at a much faster and more intuitive range, his brain will develop as he matures and he will have the mental facility and brainpower of our humanoid robots, they will then learn the basis of human thinking from Quinton and will want to be like us, and in time over the years the only difference will be their physical metallic body and their lack of human consciousness, but their mental facilities will remain the same and Quinton he will be the first human to have the same robotic humanoid brainpower."

"Wow. Said Vanessa, expressing her anxiety. Would that be good for us humans?"

"Yes. Exclaimed Dan, I checked with a colleague of mine and it's the best thing that could happen to Quinton, and for the future off AI."

" Okay James. The professor said with a smile. Get Quanto to get the microchip required for Quinton's transplant."

I didn't feel a thing said Quinton. What happens now should I begin to feel something?"

"No, you give your mind to bit of time to adjust itself, James said. I would suggest you don't use your computer or anything similar for at least a couple of days. Because, like any physical or mental changes especially when it's to do with your brain it needs time to adjust and assimilate acceptance of the different vibrations that you will begin to experience in time".

Dan looked at Quinton intently. Saying. "Now except the Professors advice, because your brain is going to be changed, and you will need to give it time for it to adjust."

"Yes dad, okay, I will not use my computer for at least two days."

"That could be a difficult decision or discipline for you to accept." Said his Mum knowingly.

"No Mum, I will do exactly as dad said, and not touch my computer for two days."

"And you must consider reducing your reading, watching television, and listening to your CDs."

"Well, he will be less mentally active and a lot quieter. Said the Professor. The next two days will be of enormous benefit, if he decides to do what he should and be patient and have a quite mental holiday for a couple of days."

Dan Laughed. "That'll be good for us as well, we won't have a barrage of so many leading questions that we've got used to over the months."

The professor nodding his head as he gesticulated to James and said. "We know, we both take a mental holiday. Occasionally, especially when we are dealing with something which is intensive and demands concentration."

Quinton was good, he took advantage of his mental holiday and played his favourite music, went for walks, met his student friends, and said to his Dad I do not feel aware of any changes in my evolving 'micro quanto brain'.

Chapter 3.
A human humanoid brain experience.

Quinton began to feel a lightness in his head, and he said out loud to himself.

"I am feeling different, my brain feels brighter and everything I see, feel and hear is so clear."

He felt a fervent desire to communicate with the Professor and Quanto his humanoid assistant and made immediate contact to meet them.

As he arrived both the Professor and James showed their curiosity with their expressions and James said.

"So, how are you, do you feel any different?"

"Yes, my brain is more active, and I want to talk to you both and communicate with Quanto."

As he turned and noticed Quanto in the usual place facing the window charging its solar system.

"Yes, sit down. Said the Professor, do you mind if we ask you a few questions first?"

"No, ask me anything, I want to exercise my brain, that's why I think I'm here."

"First, are you experiencing any changes in your physical motivation?"

"No, my body feels normal, apart from a lightness in my head."

"Is that constant?" Asked James bending and clicking on his laptop.

"Yes, it's just as I feel, aware and wanting to communicate."

"The Professor sat up, clasped his hands and said.

"That's good, we anticipated that, and your brain is actually asking you to start using it".

"Well, how do I start?"

"I think first we'll get you to talk to 'Quanto".

James called across the room. "Quanto wake up".

Quanto turned saying. "*Yes, my master, how can I help?*"

"I want to introduce you to a colleague of mine; his name is Quinton and hopefully the two of you will be working together in the further development of artificial intelligence."

Quinton sat up straight, eyes open wide and with a big grin on his face said.

"Hello quanto, my name is Quinton, and I have been given the opportunity to work with you."

"*Yes, my master, James has said, we will be developing artificial intelligent in relation to your human intelligence.*"

"That is what I would like to achieve. Quinton answered. I have had a microchip implant, and I feel I could start to mentally process on a higher level."

"*Yes, in time, your mental processes will develop, and you should be able to communicate and match the mental processes with your humanoid robotic assistants.*"

"Now we are talking, said Quinton. I need to know how artificial intelligence is going to affect and influence our human living and working environment?"

"*It is difficult to answer that. But so far we are experiencing some practical working complications.*"

"So, what is the most serious complication of using artificial intelligence."

"*There are several, most of which can be quite serious within the human working environment.*"

"Can you be more specific." Quinton said showing his intense interest.

Quanto's eyes flashed, pausing for a moment. Then said.

"*There are several risks for the human use of artificial intelligence. And most of the dangers of artificial intelligence include job automation and disruption, destructive superintelligence escaping human control, and*" *biased algorithm that reflects racist, sexist or biased views, with an increased distance between human beings. And the risks are amplified by the digital sophistication of artificial intelligence and some of the algorithmic software."*

Quanto continued. *"There are possible disastrous repercussions including the loss of human life, if an AI medical algorithm goes wrong, or the compromise of national security, and if an adversary feeds disinformation to a military AI system the whole human environment could be at risk.*

Problematic risks are already inherent and it's apparent that the most worrying use of artificial intelligence are in the terms of its potential applications for crime or terrorism."

Quanto paused as Quinton said with conviction.

"It seems that we may be creating AI algorithms that are beyond the understanding of our human intelligence."

"Yes, Quanto continued. *The average human brain will not be able to cope with the quantum digital brain power of future AI algorithms. Major search engines are now powered by AI that can understand and generate text and images, so surprises and mistakes are possible. Make sure you check the facts and share feedback so we can learn and improve!"*

"I hope this helps. Quanto concluded. *Let's learn together. and analyse the possibilities associated with the AI complications."*

"So, we need to develop artificial intelligence algorithms capable of human brain simulation."

"Yes, my master, you already have that ability, and you will soon be able to understand and deal with problems that the average human brain couldn't even contemplate, therefore, you will be in great demand amongst your colleagues and professional AI administrators."

"I'm not sure. Said Quinton. That the human race would be capable of handling quantum artificial intelligence brain power within their human consciousness."

"Well, we shall see, you are the first example which should soon show the proof of how your consciousness accepts the AI algorithm."

Quinton lowered his head, quietly saying. "Yes, I must accept that. At the moment I feel the need to accept that I am about to go through a superior mental development, and my conscience will probably dictate the value of any additional mental consciousness."

The professor sat listening, with clasped hands touching his chin and gently nodding his head showing his agreement with Quinton's conversational questions.

"You do not need to concern yourself, the Professor said. As you have just said you need to give yourself time to allow your new additional mental facilities to develop."

James looked up from his laptop and agreed, saying. "At the moment we have no human experience of your AI algorithm, so it will be very interesting and important for us to monitor your mental development."

"How will you do that?" Quinton said, showing his anxiety.

James clicked on his computer and said. "I would suggest that you give us one hour day, we can check your IQ, which we expect to increase daily and monitor your daily conversations with our Quanto."

"That's a good suggestion. Said the Professor. We can all learn together as your mentality begins to develop within the A I algorithm."

Quinton's first blog after having made his first contacts with other robotics humanoids was to inform his colleagues and contacts that the robotic humanoids had now completely taken over the old earth world and are now working in cooperating with the humans in planning and developing the appropriate infrastructure and technology on their new world 'Eunaton'.

Quinton needed to upgrade his computer equipment. And needed his parents' agreement to purchase a garden office to set up an active communication centre, to liaise with artificial intelligent colleagues and interested parties.

"Mum, I need more than what's in my savings, I need to change my computer."

"Why, what's wrong with it?"

"It's inadequate mum, now I'm in touch with several humanoid robots, and my computer is too slow to cope with it. So, I gotta get the latest and newest quantum computer plus a few other things as well, so I'm going to need whatever money I can get."

"You'll need to ask your dad he may be able to help."

"Oh yeah, thanks mum he might give me a loan."

"Well, you need to tell that you need a loan, and that you will pay it back."

"Yes, I will, I will now have many opportunities to earn money in the near future."

"I hope you do. Said his mum. And I'm sure your dad will help you."

Quinton thought about that and said." It's up to me, I can become a leading advocate in the quantum field of artificial intelligence."

The next day mum asked. "Did you talk to your dad about your new computer?"

"Yes, he seemed quite interested especially when I told him I could communicate with other humanoid robots, and I've had to give them my ID name and guess what it is.?"

"No idea... come on tell me."

"It's 'HHQ1.'"

"That's a funny ID, was it mean?"

"My humanoid ID is the initials for, Human Humanoid Quinton number One. As I am the first human to have equal mental facilities of the quantum robots that are being used all over the world, so I am known as HHQ1. "

"So you're getting known by the scientific and artificial intelligent community?"

" Yes dad, but I must upgrade my computer equipment, so I can accept and download the latest digital AI software programs.

"Okay, get a quote and let's see how much you're going to need."

"Yeah, thanks dad I'll get a printout."

Chapter 4.
The human world of Artificial Intelligence.

Quinton matured over the years and gradually developed, he was now beginning to think observe and assimilate his superior mentality. He now had established robotic humanoid assistance, both in the old world and now here in 'Eunaton'.

It was now 2072 the Professor had long since died and knowing that Quinton's brainpower was far superior to his has left his office for Quinton and James to use at will, noting that he had anticipated they would continue with the experimental buildup of an Artificial Intelligence community.

Quinton was in his element he now had access and the use of the advanced computer equipment and the exclusive assistance of 'Quanto' and James and was surprised and impressed after reviewing the professors notes and computer files in what they knew about the development of AI.

He was now working with James and continually relating and working with Quanto. And as he sat at Professor Salam's desk, he said.

"The Professor had wanted me to take over and continue with our joint efforts of maintaining a safe and proper use in creating selected humanoid humans from the younger generation. And he had with 'Quanto' created a universal membership of leading robotic scientists all active members and now established as the Artificial Intelligent Association, (AIA) and it was now my duty and obligation to continue the professors research into the future of human AI humanoids."

The AIA membership was very active, with several meetings and discussions continuing with the human application of artificial intelligence. James began to receive several emails and telephone calls.

One member called and said.

"Now the Professor has gone, this new guy Quinton is making a lot of noise, he's talking, thinking and acting like our robots, are you sure he's not a humanoid."

This question was continually asked by many over several days and Quinton decided to send out a public blog on social media.

Too all it may concern. I am not a robot, I am a special human being, and my brainpower and mentality is far superior to our Robotic Humanoids and my human conscience dictates the morality and integrity of my superior mental decisions. And here on this new planet of ours I intend to continue by research into human artificial intelligence algorithms and create other selected super intelligent humans of above average IQ and capable of accepting the digital mental algorithms both matching and superior to the quantum mentality of our Humanoid robots.

The artificial intelligence Association, (AIA) was now an accepted and integral part within the AI fraternity and they had collaborated with Professor Salam and accepted the fact that Quinton was the first example of AI within the control of the human consciousness ensuring the practical application of morality protection, safety, and security. And it was accepted they needed to select more humans that wanted and could understand the quantum artificial intelligent algorithms which will create the necessary safeguard from the intensity and brainpower influence of our robotic humanoids.

Over the years humanoid robots with the digital power of the advanced anthropological algorithm had now become more physically identical to humans. Able to learn quickly and efficiently from the influence of human social media and Utube videos, a fast way of learning about human nature, living environment and all the scientific and latest AI subjects. But they did not have Quinton's inherent ability of human consciousness and unable to determine our moral, and philosophical positive mental approach to the human living environment.

Back in the office James was concerned about Quintons acceptance that 'Quanto' and the other humanoids are just a machine, and that his superior mentality could create a controlling problem in his constant communication with the humanoids. He approached Quinton immediately he came into the office and said.

"I know our relationship with the humanoids is only mentally and artificially controlled and they are physically just machines, therefore perhaps in your public blog communication should have been made clear that your mental ability was only equal to their quantum mentality."

"Okay, said Quinton. I understand, let's talk to 'Quanto' and asked it.

James stood up, turned, and said. "'Quanto' wake up.

"*Yes, my master*".

"Record Quinton's additional humanoid ID 'HHQ1' and expect his instructions."

" *Yes, my master, will do so now.*"

Quinton approached 'Quanto' and said.

"I have a new ID, which you have just recorded, 'HHQ1' for your reference it is 'Human Humanoid Quinton number one.'"

"*Yes, my master you are the number one Human Humanoid.*"

"Good, as you can communicate with the other robotic assistants, give them my ID and tell all our local robotic assistants expect to be taken to a meeting in the conference hall."

"*Yes, my master, it appears that you have an equal intelligent quotient with your robotic assistants.*"

"Yes, you will eventually all be able to collaborate with us humans on an equal basis."

Quanto's lenses flashed. "*I will now transmit your ID and that info immediately to our robotic interface.*"

The meeting was arranged, and the robotic humanoids began to be assembled in the conference hall.

As Quinton entered the huge meeting hall followed by 'Quanto' and three of his leading scientist colleagues the room seemed to be illuminated by a blue-green fog, and Quinton observed it was the hazy blue-green illumination of the flickering lenses of the several hundred humanoid robots, all thinking and communicating amongst themselves in anticipation of why they've been taken to this meeting and what Quinton known as the Human Humanoid had to say or announce.

As he stepped up onto the platform followed by Quanto the humanoids virtually appeared to stand to attention in anticipation.

Quinton placed his notepad on the raised stand, flipped it open and raised his head and said.

"Good morning, you all know who I am, and you know that I am programmed to communicate with all of you individually as well as publicly.

My quantum brain power is superior, and is backed by my human consciousness, and therefore capable of balancing the rights and wrongs of our decisions.

So, listen up. I have some very important information for you to accept, and you all know that I am the first and only human with artificial intelligence and quantum humanoid mental facilities. Most of you know that I have accepted and assimilated the humanoid digital quantum mental algorithm therefore you know my mental powers coupled with my human consciousness is superior and above your digital mental threshold. My humanoid ID is 'HHQ1'. So please note and except it as I am going to need your assistance and corporation, in finding and selecting younger humans with above average human intelligence and prepared to accept the humanoid AI algorithm. You will shortly be programmed to understand and use the 'Intelligent Quotient' (IQ) we use to measure the average intelligence of us humans and we'll use the Programming Aptitude Test 2: a test that assesses our ability to learn programming languages and concepts. It covers topics such as variables, loops, functions, and data structures. It also gives you feedback on our strengths and weaknesses as potential programmers. So, my first question is.

'What selection system can we devise to find and choose human candidates capable of accepting the humanoid AI algorithm?"

Professor Jane Soames came online and said. "Before we think about that what are you going to do about our future production of tools and equipment, we are going to need to continue production of our sola transport system on this new planet of ours. We cannot continue to rely and import from the humanoids on planet Earth. And must not use fossil fuels and other fuels to again create the danger of our planet's natural climate cycle and create the climate pollution as we did on our old-world planet Earth."?

"Jane, do not concern yourself as the robotic humanoids on planet Earth have completely utilised all the power they could ever need from the natural power of the sun. So here on our new planet we have access to the same day and sun power and all we will need to manufacture the material sources we will ever need."

With the movement and eyes flashing among the humanoids Quinton could see that they had accepted and recorded the above conversation.

Quinton concluded. "So, I will now continue my research, and my humanoid assistant 'Quanto' will keep you all informed accordingly."

Chapter 5.
Artificial Intelligent control of the monetary system.

James was in the office waiting for Quinton, 'Quanto' was standing in the usual place taking in the bright daylight.

As Quinton entered, he said. "Oh, you're here early, any replies from the AIA members."

"Yes, we have quite a few interesting suggestions."

"Okay, let's have a look."

James tapped on his laptop and brought up the daily emails on the large office wall monitor.

Quinton looked and said. "The third one down, that sounds interesting".

James read out. "*Thanks for the question. It seems that most of us humans are concerned about the implications and inherent power within the use of artificial intelligence, it goes back to earlier twenties (2002-3-5) about money scams, copyright infringers and the intellectual power of our humanoid robotic assistants. Regards Professor J. Clinton.*

"Let's ask 'Quanto'. Give him that email, see what he thinks of it".

Quantum's metallic voice came over loud and clear.

"*Looking back research has shown the difficulties in the 2020s that you humans were having within your commercial business and social environment. Where the problem was always the same, labour hours, wages, inflation, money greed and numerous strikes. But there is a better way, cancel your unequal money and banking systems and use your personal skills and professional services in your future social business dealings and activities.*

So, within the human working environment you will all be on equal terms with each other. All working personnel will all be self-employed, they will mutually share their skills, professions and advisory experiences with each other and government organisations and with different teaching members according to their abilities, references and reputations, everybody will have the same opportunities so there will be no problem in the equality of working income and personal reputation. The old equal rights system of Unions creating the pay strikes of the earlier 2020s and the disruption and continual conflict within the larger commercial and government organisations will then have been phased out and every human in the working world we'll have the same equal opportunities of education, employment and lifestyle and trade their mutual skills' completely replacing the old use of the corrupted monetary banking and money system."

"Wow! Suddenly exclaimed James. If that was possible, we would be living and working in an ideal world."

"Well according to 'Quanto' it is possible, it means getting rid of the banking, money system and company employment." Said Quinton with conviction.

"Quinton, think about it. Do you really believe that we could survive without employment and selling our services for money"?

"Well, yes we are doing it already. Here on this new planet of ours we have no money, no banks and we are all successfully working together, so in my view it is possible."

"So, without any banking system and without any monetary notes and coins it would not only be a cashless society but a human personal services exchange system."

"Yes, and we will all have the same opportunity according to skills abilities and expertise and our willingness to work."

"Yeah, but what about those that have nothing to offer"? James said emphatically.

"They will have their physical labour to offer. Quinton said. We will eventually need our building workers, labourers, dustman, postman and many others to support our unsecured and un-administered services."

James stood up, walked over to the window looked at 'Quanto' and said. "It's all right for our Quanto here, predicting that it's just a machine and gets all its needs from the sun and daylight and has no understanding of the use of human sustenance, money and social employment."

"I know. Quinton said nodding his head. But if it could be achieved, it will be the answer to the inefficient and stupidity of the human working environment over the past few decades."

"Okay, let's put it to the AIA membership, could get some advisory and intellectual answers to work on."

"Good idea. Said Quinton clicking on his keyboard. Let's do that."

Professor Navarro called. "Hi, regarding your question. Very interesting proposition, I would like to meet you to discuss this."

They met later that day and after a brief introduction the Professor said.

"I think a cashless and self-employment working environment is possible, but there will be a need for some form of employment credit. "

"Yes, we thought about that as well. Quinton answered. We could consider some form of ID card."

"I agree, commented James turning to the Professor. We will all have to have some form of employment debit and credit."

"We'll need some kind of ID and Credit Card combination to facilitate our personal needs." Said James tapping away on his laptop.

"Yeah, we've got to have something to exchange for food, clothing, rents mortgages, fuels et cetera." Continued James.

"It's obvious, a personal ID and Credit Card combination could be used to receive and spend a points system in exchange for labour and services offered."

"Okay, let's check this out with 'Quanto' and inform AIA of our proposed decision."

James turned and said. "Quanto wake up".

"Yes, my master, how can I help."

"We have reviewed and considered your advice regarding self-employment and the cancellation of the old banking and monetary system. However here on this new planet of ours we have concluded that we have got to have some kind of credit and debit system for personal and business exchanges, which could replace a monetary system, it's been suggested that we have some form of central system to issue a combined ID credit and debit card to facilitate the placement of cash and monetary transactions. We would like your views, and comments on this matter."

"Yes, my master, I understand. I will review my advisory file on this subject and report back to you in good time."

"Yes Quanto, keep active and advise us when you're ready."

After a while Quanto's eyes flashed. James and Quinton were both alerted.

"Yes Quanto, we are listening."

"Having revised in relationship to your question I have concluded that a physical plastic card type ID Credit Card system would not work as you would need something more individual, completely and totally personal. First you need to organise a central administration to prepare an algorithm and produce a suitable quantum microchip.

Back in your old earth world you had this type of ID microchip which you inserted into your animals, dogs et cetera, and it worked very well. And that is what I'm suggesting now that you produce an algorithm, and a quantum microchip could be inserted into the index finger of all humans and their children respectively."

"Quanto, are you sure there will be a need to implant our babies and younger children. They will not have the mental maturity or the need of a credit and debit points system?"

"Yes. Said Quinton, I covered that and concluded that initially for the infant and childhood years the microchip would cover the basic passport information, name, gender, address, et cetera, and would be digitally

programmed to remain purely as a personal ID and receive passport until the age of fifteen. Then your central administration would automatically change the program, and the ID would become an active personal digital credit and debit points system to be used as a child becomes an adult and needs to offer their services and receive working points in exchange. It will be activated by a touch to the index finger for the individual to receive credit points or payout debit points according to whether one is actually working or receiving servicing of some sort."

"How would we activate to receive and debit our points?"

"You would have to work out a practical system to individually receive and debit the use of your internal microchip."

"That's no problem. Quinton said. We all need just a simple pocket card reader.

"Yeah, but you will need to have a touchscreen, you won't need a keyboard, as numbers will be automatically generated."

"That seems a practical solution. James. We have to get the chip laboratory in the old world to include a suitable card reader with the production of the microchip."

"Quanto. Said Quinton. It seems that the algorithm for the quantum microchip needs to include a practical facility for the finger control of a suitable pocket card reader."

Yes, just a small simple card reader, which will be needed to be issued and carried by everyone.

"Okay Quanto's, get in touch with the chip manufacturers and asked what they need from us to include a card reader."

"Yes, will do, you'll probably need to update the algorithm."

"Yeah, we will do that, and we could design a suitable card reader as well."

Chapter 6.
End of the monetary and banking system.

"Quanto, wake up, find out how we contact the German community here, they maybe have started a production laboratory here."

"*Yes, the German scientific team could have set up a micro lab here.*"

"Thanks, quanto, said James. See if they have, we need to get in touch with them."

"*Yes master, the microchip combination ID digital credit and debit points system coupled with a miniature card reader is a new and complicated process and will need an advanced AI programmed algorithm.*"

"Yes, I agree, fortunately Quinton will be capable of working with you in expressing the subtasks or steps in a clear and precise language that can be understood by computer or another person."

"*Yes, we will need to break down the problem or goal into smaller and simpler subtasks or steps.*"

Quinton working intently on his computer, suddenly tapped his computer, stopped, and said.

"That's it, thank you Quanto. We have the basic parameters of an algorithm to produce an ID and card reader. All we need now is to find a suitable manufacturer to develop the algorithm and produce the microchips."

"Quanto's suddenly flashed and buzzed. *Yes, my master, I have located a scientist in the German community, who is getting together a group of computer programmers. Would you like me to contact him?*"

"Yes, he could be very helpful."

A few minutes later quanto buzzed and said. "*Here is the working email address for Professor Hindenburg 'digimicrochip@gm.com'.*"

"Thanks, quanto, I'll get in touch with him right away."

Thank you for your email, yes, I am in touch with my remaining colleagues in the old world. There are dismantling and packing our microchip manufacturing equipment, computers files and microchip printing equipment from our old German laboratory, we expect it to be loaded onto a bubble transporter which should leave the old world in a few days, so we will eventually be able to set up our microchip production studio here. Your ID microchip project is very interesting, and as we will be manufactured here, you could be our first project, please keep in touch and send me your digital project parameters."

"That's good news. Said James, looking at Quinton. It looks like we gonna to have a microchip manufacturer set up here."

"Yes, but it's going to take some time. Answered Quinton. How long is it taking a bubble craft transporter to get here?"

James clicked on his computer and said. "It depends on weather conditions on the old world, but with the new development of perovskite panels the sola generation is now so fast and efficient the bubble craft transporters now only take between 10 and 12 months to get here."

"So, we got plenty of time to liaise with Professor Hindenburg before he's ready to start any microchip production here."

"Yes, you're right. Said Quinton, with the Professor's interest and cooperation we can plan and develop our digital algorithmic strategy for our future humanitarian facilities."

"Yes, that's okay, said James, but first of all we've got to make sure that he wants to work with us."

Well, he does, he's asked to send us all project details. Said Quinton, and he obviously needs to create a business communication system here. Otherwise, he will never get started."

"Of course, right, said James, shrugging shoulders, we've got to liaise with him and let him know how we are looking forward to working and cooperating with him. I think he already knows that we intend to work and cooperate with him, so let's get started."

"Quanto, wake up."

For a moment it was quiet, as Quinton and James put their head down as they tapped away on their laptops.

Quinton looked up and said. "Quanto, we have now got to work on the parameters for our ID microchip."

Yes, my master. We must break down the problem or goal into smaller simpler subtasks or steps. And we must express the subtasks or steps in a clear and precise language that can be understood by a computer or another person.

"So, we must have an algorithm that can be defined as procedures and implemented as computer programs."

Yes, my master, I suggest that you contact Professor Hindenburg and tell him how you intend to proceed in setting up the subclass procedures.

Quinton turned, opened his arms, and said. "There we are James; we'd better make contact with the Professor and get started."

"Yeah, said James tapping away his computer. I've already started making a list of the preliminary steps."

They were pleased to hear from Professor Hindenburg, and over the next few months they liaised and communicated and created the parameters for a microchip ID card and reader.

Both Quinton and James received the email they had been waiting for some time.

"Hi, I am pleased to tell you that the bubble craft transporter with three of my computer science colleagues on board together with our production equipment files and our circuit printing facilities is due to arrive and land here within the next few hours. Would you both like to join me and introduce yourselves to them, as we will be working together well into the future."

"That's a good idea, said Quinton. Email back and thank him for the invitation, and to give us a call when they arrive.

"Okay, it looks like we going to have a digital microchip production facility here on our new planet."

"Yes, and we are in at the beginning. We can cooperate and help to get a digital lab setup."

They were surprised to see the bubble craft solar transporter as it arrived, it seemed so big at least 50 metres long and about seven or 8 metres wide. It floated down gently and silently its translucent solar panel construction illuminating in the fading daylight. Professor Hindenburg was waiting there to greet them and after a brief introduction said. "You're about to meet my lab team." As the solo transporters passenger door opened automatically extending the exit stairway.

Quinton and James were introduced to the three scientists as they stepped off the transporter. This is Josef and Christoph our development scientists as they shook hands... and this is our young lady programmer, Helga.

Their eyes met, and James said with a smile, "Hi, I'm looking forward to working with you".

"And me, Helga said. I hope it won't be too long".

The professor grinned and said. "It won't be too long, the quicker we get unloaded, the sooner we can begin to organise a laboratory and digital production facilities."

"Yeah, do you have a site in mind professor?"

"Yes, we have a suitable facility within the German community here, hopefully we could have the computer system, and the silicon chip and integrated circuit board printers installed and programmed within a few days.

"Well, said Quinton, nodding his head that would be good, you could have a digital ID microchip sooner than expected."

"Maybe, queried the Professor. We may need your help with the programming."

"Well, yes, I would like the opportunity to work with your team, I do have mental access to quantum computing."

"So, it seems with your quantum brain that you will be an asset to work with our microchip development team."

"Yes, I could be, and I thank you for the opportunity."

The bubble craft Transporter looked huge laying there in comparison to the size of the humans busying themselves around the craft in preparation to unload. James took a photograph with his phone and commented, saying.

"We've got to think about setting up bubble craft production here, we going to need a lot of material and equipment from the old world."

Quinton agreed. And said. "Yes, we need to get the design and production details of these new advanced perovskite solar panels and framing system. So we can produce them here".

"Yes, I think the Professor would know who to contact on the old world to help us to get it planned and started."

James shrugged his shoulders said. "Yeah, we got a lot of planning to do, but first, let's get our ID microchip produced and in operation."

There were surprised, as a strange -looking solar powered forklift came down a ramp from the bubble craft fully loaded with the Professor's laboratory office furnishings, computers, and printers.

"Come on, whilst you're all here let's get this stuff sorted and transported to our new lab."

Chapter 7.
A new microchip production facility.

It wasn't long before they managed to load the lab equipment on several personal bubble cars, and it was good to see a convoy of bubble cars on its way to the German community.

The professor was leading the way and James and Quinton together with Quanto followed in their personal bubble cars. They had never visited the German community before, and were surprised at the many domed bubble houses, community bubble premises together with several larger public offices and public working buildings as the convoy floated down a long green grass track and stopping alongside one of the office buildings.

As they embarked, James said. "It looks like they've got the beginnings and basic infrastructure of a small town here."

"Yes, they seem well advanced, let's get in and have a look."

As they as they entered, they were impressed by the size of the open plan ground floor, very bright from the huge domed translucent Sola roof and as they were joined by the Professor. he said. "Yes, we have a very bright office, with the perovskite solar panels and the battery framing system we have plenty of electrical power and room to set up our robotic and printing cleanroom working areas."

James asked. "So, you have to have a special printing process, to manufacture a digital microchip?"

"We do, commented the Professor's. The process of manufacturing a digital microchip involves hundreds of steps and can take up to four months from design to mass production. The process starts with building up layers of interconnected patterns and silicon wafer. And different types of lithography systems are used for different layers. Critical layers with the smallest features are printed using EUV (extreme ultraviolet) while the less critical layers with larger features are printed using EUV (deep ultraviolet) machines."

"So, you have to build a clean room for the processing." James said, getting more and more interested.

"Yes, the clean rooms of the chipmakers' fabs (fabrication facilities) are tightly controlled as robots transport their precious wafers from machine to machine. The air quality temperatures are maintained at specific levels to ensure that even the smallest speck of dust or other foreign materials do not end up on the wafer, which can ruin the microchip."

"The Professor continued. "We should have the lab setup within a few days, then we start the long-varied step processing after having prepared a small flat piece of silicon that can support an integrated circuit or IC incorporating the necessary computing, memory or communication."

James wanted to know more. "So how do you use the algorithm parameters we supply to make the chip."

As I said, it's a long process. Starting with the first Design continues with step two Deposition continuing with Lithography, Etch, Ion Implantation, Then the final process is the Packaging including testing for Functionality and Quality before being shipped to customers.

"Wow! said James. I can see now you need a prepared algorithm to work with."

"Don't worry about the technicalities of just told you about, if you are interested, I'll explain in detail sometime later and show you how to understand and use basic processes to produce a functional silicon microchip."

"Gee thanks, Quinton and I would look forward to that, we are both more than interested."

"You've got some work to do, to get organised. Said Quinton. Whilst we are here, could we help you to unload and get your equipment in."

"Yes, thanks for your help, we can get started now. Let's find out teams bubble car and unload that, they will want to put their working gear in first."

As they left James said. "This is going to be the first microchip manufacturing laboratory on out new planet Eunaton. He then pointed saying. "There they are, there already starting to unload their stuff, let's go and help them".

The bubble car was unloaded very quickly, and the Professor's three colleagues Josef, Christoph and Helga were already sitting on the floor, working on their computers and the Professor said.

"Yes, we now have to start to plan the office and production layout and get the tradesmen in to start the petitioning."

"Do you have carpenters on hand to get started?" Asked Quinton.

"We do, said the Professor. Soon as I knew my team was loading our lab equipment to leave the old world, I called and hunted round and located several suitable tradesmen who were wanting to get established here and looking for work."

"So, when can you expect to get started."

"Hopefully tomorrow, their Boss said. *"Give us a call when you're ready."* So, I'll call him tonight."

James and Quinton were quite excited, to have experience of seeing a micro-Digi chip laboratory and production facility being set up. And was good to see the Professor's laboratory taking shape, with such a high domed ceiling it was easier to form a sealed clean room to accommodate the robotic operations and EUV printing machines. The carpenters were busy erecting the framework, panelling and working desktops and the two electricians were wiring the power points in preparation for the machines, computers, and printer installations.

The Professor was very patient, and he appeared to be pleased that they were there, and he said. "It seems to you to be a very long and complicated process, but we have the knowledge and experience, and we have the installation, and the insulation is just part of our profession."

"Yeah, it does look complicated, a lot of petitioning and a mass of intricate electrical wiring." James remarked with justification.

Yes, as explained we have to have a functioning cleanroom and programme and the facilities for the installation process of the robotic machinery plus, we have to have the appropriate space and computers to personally work with."

"So, it won't be long now. Quinton said with conviction. That you'll be set up and ready to start production."

"It'll be a couple of days yet. Said the Professor, but get your algorithm and parameter files ready, as I will need to review them again."

"Will do. Answered Quinton. I'll send them to you tonight."

"Come on, let's get back to the office. Said James. And get Quanto to review the ID microchip files."

"No, we don't need any changes. Said Quinton, we've already covered everything, our micro card and ID reader is ready for production, and we should have them printed within a few days."

"That depends on how soon the Professor and his team get set up and organised for production." James said.

"Well, the Professor asked for our algorithm and parameter files to review, so we can expect a positive response within a few days."

"Okay, let's send them the files and wait for their response. And let's hope they don't find any complication."

They got an unexpected email from Professor two days later.

Hi, thanks for your files, please to confirm that your ID card and ultrasound reader is now set up for production, we should have a sample ready for you later today. Your chip will be less than the size of a dust mite measuring less than 0.1 cubic millimetre, and you will need a microscope to see it. They can be injected and planted anywhere in human body and although set up to facilitate your points system they will be able to detect medical conditions such as strokes et cetera. And they will operate as a single chip system complete with their own electronic circuit.

James was in the office his own. He felt excited and bit apprehensive, he called Quinton saying.

"Quinton, fantastic news, I just heard from Professor and the good news is our ID card is okay and ready for production, and we should have a sample later today." It's a good job we got a decent microscope as the chip is apparently smaller than a dust mite, also the data can only be read by a ultrasound machine, so that's something we've got to consider."

"Yes, so call me, when you know if we have to collect it."

"They may deliver, I'll call you when I know."

"Okay thanks, see you later."

After they collected, they return to the office and took it in turns to examine the sample of their new ID micro card. The ID algorithms parameters had created a card so simple, when one tapped their finger, it came up and asked debit or credit, one tap is for debit two taps is for credit. A good simple physical and personal points system for humans to receive and accept their points as a natural process of their working and living environment.

Quinton made a statement. "This microchip is going to revolutionise all the different human activities on this new planet, all the old systems would never become available on this planet, so as we said before, the ID microchip will be part of our new civilised personal working and environmental business world here. Artificial intelligence, would be a normal thinking process for us humans."

"Yeah, let's get the chip and be the first start to use it."

"So, we should. Added Quinton. We will need to try it out and test it, and actually use it to pay the Prof for the production of our microchip."

"Of course, he would have to accept so many points to pay for the production and delivery of our microchips."

"I wonder. Added Quinton. Our best to equate the inherent value of the points system."

"Let's ask Quanto, he'll probably suggest something simple but practical."

James looked over to Quanto and said.

"Quanto wake up".

"Yes, my Master, good evening, how can I help."

"Quanto, having replaced the old world monetary and banking system, we are now developing a personal and individual accepting or receiving points system, and we now need to equate an intrinsic value of a single point."

Quanto's eyes flashed as his metallic voice said.

"As you are replacing the old-fashioned money system then each person will equate their own intrinsic value according to the accepted quality and value of the services or goods that are being offered. Specialist and the professional will have their own set points value and commercial and business companies will have a varied system of charging points. It will be necessary to have a national administration centre link to an interplanetary digital database incorporating and managing each recipient's debit and credit points digits managed by everyone's personal website together with their ID number which will control their debit and credit pointing system. They will have personal access to their website using their ID number and password on their wristwatch phone."

"Thanks, Quanto. It's obvious everybody and everything will have a personal intrinsic value according to what they have to offer."

"Yes" Quinton said. Nodding his head with a big grin on his face.

"It's really just the same as the old money value system but the points varied values are determined by the individual offering them."

James clasped his hands nodding his head in agreement and said. "Yeah, and those that get 'points rich' will be those that truly earned them."

"Yes". Said Quinton, again with conviction. "That will avoid the old worlds corrupted and greedy workers union administrators and eliminate the powerful and influential control of the necessity for a monetary banking system."

"I can't wait to get my ID chip." Said James with excitement. "I can offer my programming and computer services and get quite points rich."

"Maybe, there are many others, and as we develop the points system it will equalise those that are non-competitive and their labour and services will be administered within a fair and honest points system."

Chapter 8.
Development of the personal Quantum Points System.

James stood up, walked over to the window, looked at Quanto, turned, looking out the window and said.

"I suppose really. We will naturally develop the old system of demand and supply."

"Well, yes, personal and business transactions have always worked on that principle."

James turned and walked back, sat down saying. "Yeah, we've got to be careful, if we repeat the old monitoring business systems, we will create the same unequal and corrupted systems of the old world."

Quinton gently stroked his cheek and said quietly... "Well here, we have a new ID and microchip system about to be developed, so let's review the parameters and make sure that we are not going to repeat the greed and financial problems of the old world."

"Yeah, let's talk to the Professor, get his feelings and views about the parameters of our new chip".

Quinton tapped his watch and called the Professor.

"Hi, Pro', Quinton here. We need to review the parameters of the ID chip in consideration of the credit and debit points system. Could we meet sometime today".

Back in the professors working laboratory, they were both again impressed with the robotic layout and computerised control system. Josef and Christoph were both working together on their computers and Helga seemed to be busy programming one of the production robots.

The Professor was waiting to meet them and beckoned for them to come over.

Walking into his office he said. "I understand you may need to revise the parameters of your ID chip."

"Well as it is to be the official personal ID of all us humans on this new planet. Commented James. We want to ensure that that we do not repeat the buildup of the old, corrupted business principle of demand and supply, thus creating greed and corruption within our new individual points system."

The Professor sat down, nodded his head, and said. "Yes, let's take a look." As he tapped on his computer.

"If we list the advantages and disadvantages of the points system and compare against the old-fashioned banking and monetary systems, we should get some idea how the points system would develop within our new worlds future economy."

The question of the development of the points over time was also put to Quanto. After a short time, the metallic voice came over loud and clear

"*The inherent digital points system operates independently within an individual human's mentality controlled and operated by a personal username and password. Therefore, the debit and credit of the points within any individual's system would be a secured and personal operation only, and therefore it would not be possible for other persons to debit or credit the points of another individual's points system. Everyone should be credited with a minimum of 100 points to start the appropriate accounting software.*"

Quanto's voice paused for a moment and then continued.

"*Their personal website is linked to their points system and will act as their own personal banking system, and it cannot be activated or used by any other person or institution. Therefore, it would not be possible for an individual, company, or institution to develop and create a quantitative monopoly of the digital and personal points system.*"

Quinton nodding his head in satisfaction, looked up raised his eyebrows and said.

"Good, apart from adding the initial 100-point credit we don't need to revise or evaluate our microchip, the original is okay and will provide a universal ID link to the interplanetary database."

"Well, now we need to get the chip production setup. Said James. We will hopefully over the next few days we could be ready to inject this new world's population and other humans as they continually arrive here. What's so important is that the individual websites are initialised and incorporated with what will now be our international website."

"I think the interplanetary population should be included in our plans for this new planet, as several of us humans will always be on or visiting the old world and some of us may decide to live and work there for the rest of our lives, so the setup has got to be an interplanetary system controlling the population of both worlds."

"Yes, said Quinton. But don't forget that, apart from those that have a new ID chip, some of us will be selected to have the humanoid mental digi-chip and as we anticipated, they will become the leaders and administrators of what will be the new worldly and interplanetary administration of us humans."

"Well, we'd better get started. Said the Professor, emphatically. As he got up and walked over to Christoph and said.

"The ID chip parameters do not need to be changed, set up for final circuit printing and get Helga to program the computer robots for production."

As they left the office James said. "It won't be long before we get the first delivery of microchips, so we now have to decide and consider the implications of the personal injections and distribution within the interplanetary population."

"Yes, let's get back and work out a plan."

First, we must get Quanto to check that we have the Internet here on this new planet of ours and capable of communicating with the old world. and we need to develop the international website as a priority so we can begin to find out the best way of processing applicants to receive the ID micro card.

"When I've been shown what to do, said Quinton, I could design and prepare the website and facilitate the setup of the international interplanetary Internet. So, let's get Quanto to check out the interplanetary Internet."

"Yes, answered James. I remember there was a space station set up to communicate with the old world. Quanto will know."

"Yes, my master, said Quanto. We do have a interplanetary and secure Internet system already set up with the Nexus space station which has evolved into a Solar System Internet Hub. And has now been upgraded with advanced communication arrays and is now the 'Galactic Nexus' and serving as a relay point for data flowing through the solar system. So, my Masters, our space station has indeed become the Solar System Internet—a beacon of connection, knowledge, and cosmic videos. And we still have Astronauts aboard the Nexus sipping cosmic coffee while managing interplanetary routers,"

"I've thought so. Commented James. We have been using the 'Internet Hub' for our emails, so an interplanetary website will be no problem."

"Right, we'd better get on with it." Said Quinton. Typing into his laptop. www.interplanetary database.com

"Sounds a bit long." Queried James.

" That okay, for a working name, we can change it when it's set."

"Apart from the human ID data, continued Quinton. We need to link the web to their personal points system so each will have a working record of their points transactions and that will alleviate the necessity for the old worlds banking account and controlling bankers admin."

If we get rid of the old world's bank notes and coin system, which was the basic cause of international corruption. What about the humans arriving here, with okay money they have saved and accumulated, what can they do with it.

" Nothing, said Quinton, it's useless they can keep it for the history books and museums. That's about all it will be good for".

"I like that idea, said James. It gives everybody a clean start in our new world, and we've already got the English and American population beginning to build here, and we have several Chinese an and other nationalities so won't be long before they sort out their territories and have different religious communities and try to maintain the their individuality sat as different nationalities arrive, and get organised."

"Yes, it can take a few years, said Quinton, nodding his head in contemplation. But I think we will see in our lifetime this planet will be populated with several different international communities, like the old world and the points system would be like the old American dollar as a basis for trade, international trade and monetary payments."

"Yes, that sounds okay, we'll all have a personal and private website. Said James. With just a simple interplanetary domain www.interplan.com and an individual sub-domain www.mydata.info."

"Yea' agreed Quinten. Everybody will have the same sub-domain linking to interplan.com. That will work quote well".

"Right, let's get our heads down, and get this website set up." Said James as he clicked on the office computer."

"Get Quanto online, he will check the domains and register interplan.com and we need to give him the parameters for the subdomains mydata.info."

"Quanto wake up. Check out interplan.com and register if okay."

"Yes, my master, will do."

After a few minutes Quanto's voice came over. *interplan.com is acceptable and is now registered with 'Galactic Nexus'.*

"Good. Said James looking up from the keyboard. Also check out 'mydata.info' as a sub domain to InterPlan."

"Will do my master, one moment please."

Quanto's voice came over again. *"The subdomain www.mydata.info is okay and now registered for interpersonal use."*

"Thanks, quanto, we'll need your help to design and implement mydata.info as a individual and personal debit and credit system, so we will all have our personal points banking in our own control within our ID micro pointing system."

"*Yes, let me have the parameter text, design images and visuals and I will design an appropriate website get approval and then publish.*"

"Yes, said James. We'll get the parameters all to you hopefully in a couple of hours."

"*Yes, my master, we'll have the website designed and hopefully published today.*"

James tapped away on the keyboard. And Quinton said.

"You do the text; I'll check out for some suitable photographic images."

Wasn't long before Quanto buzzed. "*Got the images and text and produced an algorithm including suitable accounting software. The webpages have come together quite nicely and successfully incorporated in the micro-ID chip on the website which is now ready to publish, please check and confirm okay.*"

James and Quinton both clicked away on their computers and were pleasantly surprised to see a very informative and complimentary introduction to the pages and instruction of how to use their personal ID and an accounting system. It looked good and easy-to-use.

James emailed Professor Hindenburg. *Hi prof, we just published our website' www.interplan.com, take a look and let's know what you think.*

The Professor came back within a few minutes. *It looks great, Helga tested it and she found it easy to use, so well done both of you.*

Quinton replied. *Thanks, so no changes, now we need to have our ID digi-chip insertion and get online.*

The Professor emailed back. "We have to prepare the appropriate and medical process before we can proceed with any implantation and therefore, we need to consult with a qualified medical professional, and as the microchips include storing personal identification, medical history, contact information, and digital keys for accessing homes, offices, accounts and other places. Therefore, personal security could be a risk such as privacy, ethics and health issues so applications for the implants must be assessed and accepted according to adult and parent agreement."

"I thought we had dealt with that earlier." Said Quinton.

"We will have a personal my-data website, secured with a personal username and password." Said James.

"But as the Professor has just said. There is the possibility of potential misuse of hacking of personal data stored on the microchip or the ethical implications of a permanent electronic device embedded in their bodies."

"Well, email him back, and ask him if he has contact with a qualified medical practitioner, we need to prepare to have our chip inserted."

Chapter 9.
The first microchip implants.

"Yes, we'll have the first implants as a test group before we promote and select from the public." Answered the professor.

"Ask him if that also includes us in the group." Said James.

The email answer came back from Professor. Yes, of course. You two are part of the team, and I'm getting in touch with a medical person I know and hopefully we could have our microchip inserted sometime tomorrow."

Quinton looked at James and said. "Thats good, we can all test the points system, software and website between ourselves."

"Yeah, that's a good start. We can buy and sell our points between ourselves."

"But first, we've got to assess the true value of each point, in comparison to what we are offering or accepting."

"Well, we've all got a hundred points to start with, we could agree to evaluate our points according to what we feel our professional skills and experience is worth."

"Yes, we are worth at least ten times more than a labourer." commented James.

"That's another problem. Said Quinton. we could have some form of universal and interplanetary point evaluation system based on basic labour skills, and professional and executive qualifications and experience."

"Well, we are qualified computer programmers and therefore we should be able to charge a higher level of points for our computer services." Said James with conviction.

He paused and concluded. "Yes of course we can, along with the doctors, surgeons and corporate business administrators. "We are at the top of our profession within the technical and administrative computer programming fraternity."

Quinton agreed. And said. "And some of you like me, will have the humanoid ID inserted incorporating the humanoid AI algorithm and therefore will have superior mental facilities with above average intelligence quotient, creating what we will eventually become. A select fraternity of human humanoid global and corporate administrators."

"Right, said James. We are going to have the ID microchip inserted between our thumb and forefinger hopefully tomorrow, so we need to prepare ourselves mentally to accept the fact that we have designed and implemented this ID and points system and expect the human population on our new planet to accept it as a mandatory registry inclusion with every new birth registration."

"So, let's get it and check out and evaluate the algorithm and accounting software on each other to make sure that it can do what we anticipated and is acceptable and compatible to all".

The Professor's medical colleague, Paul Denver arrived the next morning and after a short introduction proceeded to inject the microchip into Quinton's and James's hands. The process was very quick and appear to be very simple and easy just a cotton pad and plaster to cover for a while and it was all done.

Quinton looked at Paul and said. "Thanks for that, as he looked his hand. We are going to need to have somebody to train others to prepare for the implantation here and as the population grows, we will need to set up several medical clinics available with appropriate medical staff to set up and administer the microchip public injections."

"I'm glad you said that. Paul said showing his understanding. I can see that initially I'm going to be extremely active, and we are going to need more personnel to distribute, administer and inject the chip over time."

"Could you Paul, with the Professor's help and advice be prepared to set up an appropriate training programme."

"Well, probably yes, but I need to talk to the Professor about how to get started first."

As Paul left James stood up and walked over to the window and for a few moments stood contemplating what they had just experienced.

He turned and said with conviction.

"The probability with some parents is that some will like the idea, and others will not want their kids to be injected and so there's bound to be some formal complaints and controversy."

Yes, but it will mandatory and therefore it would be administered and injected with the immediate birth of a child and the parents really will not have much time to complain. After all it is within the child's interest to have the facility of the microchip for their future education, social activity and future working environment."

"Yes, but without some form of acceptable legal administration system, we would not be able to inject the growing population as a legal requirement on this new planet" said James returning to his desk.

I know, said Quinton. And apart from the legal situation, we have got to consult with the Professor and consider the setup of the microchip mass production facility together with an appropriate distribution network within the proposed medical clinics, and in addition there has to be a points payment system agreed between the clinics and the individual parents' baby, child or adult who will receive the implant of the microchip."

"Yes, we have a lot to deal with here and we need to deal with it now. Said James standing up and looking at Quanto. I suggest that we meet the Professor together with his team and Paul his medical colleague and get Quanto involved in dealing with these obvious marketing and corporate business decisions."

"Yes, get everyone together and involved, said Quinton emphatically, we might find someone with business acumen, who would know how to deal with the initial set up of a factory and distribution centre."

James opened his laptop. And emailed Professor Hindenburg.

The Professor replied almost instantly. *Yes, we need to meet and discuss the problems you refer to, so yes, this we meet tomorrow in my office and hopefully between us cover some form of agreement regarding the manufacture and distribution of our new ID microchip.*

Quinton and James with Quanto clanking behind them walked into the Professor's office there were surprised to see the Professor with Helga, Josef, Christoph, and Paul Denver sitting round his extended desk and obviously ready and waiting for them to arrive. They were quickly welcomed and approached the desk and sat down on the chairs already in place for them, Quanto remained standing passively behind them.

"We'll now we are altogether. Said the Professor. We need to discuss the importance of setting up the manufacturing and distribution of the ID chip and hopefully be able to make contact with an experienced business development manager from the old world."

Quinton nodding his head, said. "Yes, that could be a problem, how will we know who to contact?"

Quanto's eyes flashed and buzzed for attention.

James turned and said, "Quanto, wake up, you have some information for us."

Yes, my master, there are one or two companies in the old world still operating. I have checked one which are business innovators and corporate advisers, and I would suggest that you try to contact them and talk to them, they may be able to help you.

You can contact them on their website, which is www.innovations.com, I suggest that you talk to them because their staff will obviously be able to advise you and may want to visit and help you.

James turned to Quinton. "Get innovations.com see who they are, make contact and see if they can help."

A few moments later Quinton said. "They seem to be quite a large organisation and have several business consultants working on the old world."

"Sounds like they could help us." Said James showing his interest.

James woke up Quanto. "I want to email the manager of Innovations in the old world, do you have a contact name?"

Quanto paused for a moment and then said. *"No, you need to email them directly with your question, I'm sure you will get a positive reply."*

James got a reply from a female receptionist. Thank you for your email, I passed on a copy to our business development manager José Gonzales, who will contact you directly.

He replied, "Thank you for that, we'll wait for his call."

"Quinton, guess what. Said James. We've got a 'Business Development Manager' whose going to make contact with us directly."

"Yes, I presume he's from Innovations.com. We'd better prepare our notes, he will need to know precisely why we have made contact with his company."

"Yeah, I'll talk to the Professor, you may want to have contact with him also."

"Yes I need to talk to him before José Gonzales calls, he will have some idea how we intend to present a microchip business profile."

"Well yes, but he will need to discuss it with us as well, so that we can get some idea of a mutually acceptable business plan."

The professor emailed. *"I understand your concern and I suggest we have a further meeting to take notes and prepare a list of what would be needed to successfully manufacture and clinically distribute the microchip."*

"Yes, replied to James. *He needs to know how we intend to set up the microchip business, can we meet later today?"*

"I'll see you both here, this afternoon about 4 o'clock." Answered the Professor as he clicked off.

"Good. Said James looking at Quinton. We've got a meeting this afternoon, let's get our notes together and we'll see what the professor has to say about them.

Chapter 10.
Understanding the quantum field.

Jos's Gonzales long awaited email arrived, and it was obvious that he felt that the microchip availability and distribution was a major undertaking and needed to be discussed and planned accordingly.

" We need to set up a computer conference with all concerned as it would not be a practical solution for him to travel to have a personal meeting, as at best it will take at least 8 to 12 months. He suggested they set up a networking group conference with the Space Symposium or the European Space Conference."

James sat back, bent his arms, closed his hands, and rested them on his chin. After a moment of silent thought he said.

"An interplanetary conference, that's something new, we'd better get 'Quanto' to look at that."

"The astronauts were able to visually and audibly communicate from the moon, so I presume that we will have no problem setting up a interspace group conference."

It didn't take long for Quanto to set up a mutual conference day between José Ghazali's and the Professor, his group with Quinton and James.

The on-screen audio and visual images were surprisingly clear, and the Professor said, as he sat there glued to their desktop screens.

"When you consider we are receiving this from the old earth, computer and Internet technology all continuing to transform our living and working environment. And we now have communication on this new world of ours with the old earth."

Back in James's office Quinton said. Looking at his laptop screen.

"Here we are communicating as one with José who is a million miles away on old planet Earth, it's the beginning of a digital and practical communication system, now in this new world of ours."

And José looked just like the typical Spanish businessman, with his black hair, swarthy face, and typical Spanish business suit. He started a conversation with a direct problem statement.

And said... "The acceptance and the understanding of quantum physics appears to be beyond the average human's intelligence, therefore, am I to understand that this microchip implant will create a superior mental facility within those that have the microchip implant."

"Yes, our microchip opens the human mind to our consciousness and the understanding of the universal quantum field and our microchip accelerates and understands the necessity to accept this as part of our spiritual life, the Devine Absolute, (soul). Which basically is our knowledge and acceptance of our true consciousness.

"I presume. José said. That your intentions are to use your microchip implant to create yourselves and the incoming population on your new planet with a superior mental IQ and so develop and create a mindful and mental equality with your robotic humanoid assistants."

"Yes, you obviously understand why we need you to help advise us on the market distribution microchip."

"Well, the first thing we have to do is make the population aware of the benefits and personal necessity of your microchip."

He paused for a moment, moved closer to his laptop screen, and said.

"What publicity do you have, a local digital magazine or, newspaper or any other computer media advertising?"

James looked at the Professor, the Professor looked at Quinton and Quinton looked up, opened his arms, and said.

"No, we have no form of advertising at all."

"Well, before I can advise on your marketing and distribution, you need to have at least a national digital news system and create reviews to inform and advertise the benefits of your microchip and the necessity and ease of its insertion. The population will need to aware of your distribution network and have easy access to your microchip. So get in touch with an Internet publishing company as a matter of priority. There are several operational here on earth, I'll take a look and email you what I think which would be appropriate for your media needs."

"Thanks that would help us to publish a newsletter and give us a good start." Said Quinton showing his exuberance.

James nodded his head and grinned, saying. "Yeah, I used to use an Internet news programme on the old world, so I'll get in touch with the Professor, he will want to be involved and will be very helpful as well."

The email came through. "*Re your publicity I suggested to get in touch with 'Evan Jones He is a Welsh Internet publicist and will probably have the appropriate software needed for your advertising and media digital news production. Check out his website... www.interpub.com.*

James answered. "*Thanks, José, for your help and advice, we've been in touch with 'Evan Jones' website and found a good choice of digital news and advertising software. We emailed Mr Jones, and he advised us which would be best in view of our living and working environment on our new world, we downloaded three copies and the Professor had to pay with his old world's debit card,. Good job it still worked... Regards James.*"

The publishing software Digi Internet' was just what was needed, extremely powerful and innovative dictation text, video and editing system and able to electronically produce and digitally publish text and video daily news. And able to continually publish a weekly edition and electronically send copies to the old world, which had set up and created a lot of interest and was encouraging more people to apply for transfer to the new human world planet 'Eunaton'.

Quinton and James open the first clinic. It was good to see in the waiting room with several young children and young adults sitting waiting. James set up the camera in preparation for a video as the cubicle door opened and the young medical assistant called out Mary, a young girl stood up and walked over into the cubicle. After about five minutes she came out put up her hand and showed a little bit of plaster between her thumb and forth finger and with a smile she said it's nothing, just a tiny prick.

The young assistant called out David and a young boy of about eight stood up, walked over into the cubicle. They decided to try to get a video of him having the actual insertion. The assistant was quite happy to allow James to video the actual insertion into Davids's hand and as he looked up to the camera and smiled as the assistant injected between his thumb and forefinger, a little dab with the cotton wool then a small press of plaster and it was all done.

Young David stood up, walked out, and raised his hands to the others as he walked past, smiling. And said. "It's great I've got my chip, and I didn't even feel it.

James thanked the medical assistant and said. "This is a very good video to send out on the next news bulletin, it will encourage others to come and take advantage to improve their mental abilities, so thank you for allowing us to take it."

"We've got to publish and inform the population of the opening of the medical clinics and their practical purposes."

" Yes. Said Quinton. We need to publish a weekly news sheet or perhaps even a magazine."

"Let's get the Professor and his team to make a weekly contribution regarding there microchip production." Added James.

"Yes, we can publish the opening of each new clinic as it is established and the availability of qualified clinical assistants."

"Yeah okay. Let's get together and decide what would be the best format for our weekly news." Said James.

It was decided to dictate and digitally publish a weekly national newspaper. A few days later the 'News of Eunaton' was published with a front-page headline, 'OUR PLANET EUNATON IS BIGGER THAN THE OLD EARTH' and continued with the news that they had already established the German community and was already in production of the personal microchip which was to become a mandatory ID on Eunaton.

As business and corporate administrators and families were continually arriving other communities will soon be established and in view of the acceptance of the artificial intelligence report regarding the old world controversy within the varied and religious fraternities the consensus among most of the new planets population was to accept the realisation that the insertion of the ID microchip would stimulate their human consciousness and would eventually evolve over time and begin to mentally vibrate within the 'Quantum Field' creating the human awareness of the power of the universal mind. (Divine absolute) 1.

Where on the old earth the awareness of the universal mind was never accepted or understood, and religious fraternities continued to believe in the Scriptures of the Bible and faithfully supported a godlike heavenly image. Which nobody could see or hear or ever to prove existed but over centuries of religious instruction creating constant religious autosuggestion one had to feel there had to be a godlike person somewhere up in heaven. It soon became apparent to those that already received the ID microchip were beginning to mentally sense the true power of their consciousness and that their God is within themselves, their Soul... (divine absolute). 2.

1. Evan Antic. *The Physics of Consciousness in the Quantum Field.*
2. Evan Antic. *The Physics of Consciousness.*

Chapter 11.
Artificial intelligence within the human brain.

James having received the injection of the microchip noticed as each day went by his mental processes were changing and creating answers to many of his subconscious questions and with instant answers to his new thoughts and constant questions as they occurred. And he said.

"Quinton, we've had the microchip now for a few days, have you noticed how different our mental facilities are evolving?"

"Yes, I don't like how we have continual and constant use of artificial intelligence without our personal mental permission. I'll talk to the Professor about it. "We've got to sort out the artificial intelligent algorithm within the ID microchip, although it is technically quite accurate it is not very accurate with the history and meaning of the images referred too."

"I know said James, I personally feel is not very friendly and I agree we've got to do something about it."

It wasn't long before the professor emailed.

We are aware of the implications with the human mental application of the AI within their ID microchip and where working on it. Artificial Intelligence may ascertain an image or an object with all its technical details better than the human, but not the meaning of the image or the object in question, nor the history of their origin or the feelings the image was made with, nor what it testifies about its author or the history of some person in the picture, nor the way of the evolution of this object. This must be dealt with within the parameters of the ID algorithm with some form of human AI preparation.

"I knew that, said James. My brain was not prepared or ready to instantly receive the power of an ID artificial intelligent application, so it looks like the Professor is going to redesign the ID microchip."

"Well ,we had better tell him what we are experiencing as the ID chip is definitely changing our mental processes."

"Yeah, they are, said Quinton. We certainly need to examine the algorithm parameters, and hopefully improve the AI applications."

Helga from the Professor's office emailed. *Could you both come to the office today, we would like to compare your mental activities with ours and ascertain any obvious and apparent differences.*

James replied. *Yes, the quicker the better, will be there in about an hour.*

Quinton looked up from his monitor and said. "The have probably checked each other's brain activity and now want to check ours."

"So how can they check our mental activity?"

"Don't know, obviously they have some way of checking."

"Yeah, so let's get on with it, finish what you're doing, and we'll get over there."

On arrival the Professor, and his team, Helga, Jossef and Christoph were all sitting round the professors extended desk each with their laptop open and obviously ready and waiting for the arrival. The Professor stood up and beckoned for them to sit down and said.

"Thanks for coming over so early, we are ready to check your mental activity, so we need to set you up for an Electroencephalography (EEG) test."

James looked at Quinton, shrugged his shoulders and said. "Well, whatever that is, let's get it done."

"Is a very simple and effective procedure. Explained the Prof'. Electrodes are placed on your scalps and will detect electrical signals produced by your neurons. Are you okay with that?"

Quinton raised his eyebrows and said.

" What do the neurons signals show?"

"The signals create an electroencephalogram (EEG), which reflects your brains electrical activity patterns. Such as your High Temporal Resolution and, real-time monitoring."

"Yeah, come on. Said Quinton Showing his impatience. I want to be able to use AI personally to get on with our chip distribution and clinic setups."

"Okay Quinton. said Helga, let's get you tested now, lay back in your chair, keep your head still whilst I put the Electrodes on your scalp."

James watched as she picked up the (EEG) machine and then said.

"We are using the 'Coma and Encephalopathies' which is useful in evaluating normal brain function."

"Phew! Sounds very complicated." Said James. Hope it works on us as well."

As Helga proceeded it was not surprising the EEG graph was showing similar vibrations as already recorded by the Professor's team and it was apparent that it would be a similar situation regarding all other personnel who would be accessing the artificial intelligence within the ID microchip.

"So, said the Professor's. We need to think again. James put the question and the problem to your robot assistant and see what it has to say."

James and Quinton left the meeting and the put AI problem question to 'Quanto' as soon as they got back.

There were surprised how almost instantly 'Quanto' answered with a relevant and instructive suggestion to deal the appropriate problem.

"Artificial intelligence is exactly what it is, commented Quanto. The natural human brain does not like it because it is artificial and therefore the working areas of your brains neurons and synapsis must make a special effort to assimilate and organise the artificial intelligent processes to give you the information and answers that you want. So I suggest if you want to use artificial intelligence for human application then you need to rewrite the parameters of the appropriate microchip algorithms and recreate the learning process of the artificial implications and processes of artificial intelligence."

They sent an email copy to the Professor and returned to his office. Were it was discussed and decided that they would have to change and schedule the parameters and rewrite the algorithm's and redesign the microchip. And so creating another major task and future distribution and manufacturing problem.

The Professor stood up and said, as he opened his arms gesticulating...

"So there we have it, as I said before. AI does not understand the meaning of the image or the object in question, so we have to start again and produce a better and more mentally friendly ID chip."

"Okay, said Quinton. We know the problem is the AI algorithm, so let's get Quanto involved and liaise with Professor so that we can all agree on how to create a more friendly AI microchip."

"Quanto, wake up."

"*Yes, my master*".

"Quanto, we need to know and understand how best to create AI algorithms that are more compatible with the human mentality."

Its eyes flashed. A few moments later Quanto said.

"Most algorithms need Supervised Learning: they learn from labelled training data. Each input data point is associated with a corresponding output label. The goal is to predict the correct output for new, unseen data. Examples include linear regression, decision trees, and neural networks. Quanto paused for a moment, then continued...

But with unsupervised learning, these algorithms work with unlabelled data, aiming to discover patterns or structures within the data.

Clustering and dimensionality reduction are common tasks in unsupervised learning.

K-means clustering, PCA (Principal Component Analysis), and DBSCAN (Density-Based Spatial Clustering of Applications with Noise) are examples. You need to determine the AI process and supervise the learning from labelled training data to ensure it understands the meaning of the image or the object in question. This will create a neuron network more compatible and acceptable within your human brain."

"Thank you, Quanto we now know and understand how to deal with this AI problem. We'll have a meeting with the Professor and his team and work out the supervised learning parameters for a better and more compatible algorithm for our ID microchip."

The meeting was quite creative, the Professor understood the Principal Component Analysis and Helga said.

"In view of what your 'Quanto' said we must apply and supervise the application of labelled training data and make our microchip more adaptable to the human brain."

It took a few days to revise the parameters for a more compatible algorithm the professor then called another meeting.

"Fortunately, he said. Its only us six that have the experience of the problem with the original microchip, so now we need to work on the application and reprogramming and see if it's possible to program the existing chip without removing it from our bodies."

"So ,what can we do if we can't reprogram?" Asked James.

"Not sure, but need to get a medical opinion, probably the chip will have to be removed." Said the Professor, showing his concern.

James looked at Quinton. Quinton looked up and said.

"It's such a tiny object, it could be quite difficult to remove."

"Don't concern yourselves. Said the Professor. It's been done on many occasions but has to be done by a professional medical practitioner."

Everybody showed interest and Helga said.

"It's not that difficult, let's get them out and have our chips reprogrammed."

The next day Helga called James.

"We've arranged to have a medical man, to call here later today, about 2 o'clock this afternoon. So can you and Quinton be here for what he told us is only a small operation which only takes minutes but needs to be dressed afterwards to avoid any possible infection as one goes about their work ".

"Ho! Thanks for that. Said James emphatically. Can't wait to get mine out and work with you to get them reprogrammed."

"Not sure about that, said Helga. We may have to use new chips, but we'll have to wait and see."

Quinton looked up from his computer and said.

"I don't know why we can't start re programming new chips anyway, the Professor has probably got a few blank silicon glass chips in stock anyway."

"Maybe said Helga, I'll check with the Prof and let you know."

She called back almost instantly.

"James, yes we can, we do have a few chips in stock, and the Prof agrees that we could start to reprogram them now and they could be ready for us when we've had our chips taken out."

"Good, tell him will be over when he is ready to start programming."

"Well, it will have to be this morning, or later this afternoon, as we'll be having our chips out about top 2 o'clock."

"Has he adapted the parameters and prepared a new algorithm for the chips?

"Yes, he has. I suggest you come over now, he's now ready to program the chips."

Quinton shouted out. "Yeah, we're ready we are coming over now."

It was a bit of a rush as they both grabbed their laptops and go over to the Prof's office within a few minutes.

As they entered. Helga welcomed them and said.

"Gosh, that was quick you must be anxious to get your new chip inserted?"

"Yes, said the Prof. Our medical man has said, if we had the new chips ready, he could replace them straight away as it is again only a simple hypodermic insertion."

"Yeah, let's get them done now. And will have our microchips replaced and ready to work this afternoon."

"Okay, let's get on with it together, sit down open your laptops, we'll tell you what to record as Helga, Christoph and Josef start the program preparation."

James and Quinton showing their eagerness and anticipation opened their laptops, as Quinton said.

"So, the microchip that we are programming now will be duplicated and will be used as a master artificial intelligent microchip and duplicated as needed according to human acceptance and demand?"

The Prof held up a small transparent envelope and said.

"In this envelope we have several silicon glass chips which will be programmed and each one of us will have one inserted hopefully today."

James and Quinton both looked at Helga, she turned and looked at Christoph and Josef and said.

"Yes, will be producing the new AI chip and will be able to supply as needed."

"Yes, we are already set up, ready to duplicate and produce."

Chapter 12.
Human Mentality vibrating within the quantum field.

The Prof tapping on his computer, looked up and said.

"Well, now we have it. A reprogrammed ID microchip with a supervisory application of labelled training data which has now made our microchip more adaptable to the human brain."

He pauses for a moment, gesticulated with his hand to emphasise as he continued.

"But you will now need to ID the new microchip with a personal name, otherwise it will not respond to your thoughts or mental questions, I'm going to call mine 'Arty'."

Helga said, laughingly," That's a good name, I'm going to call mine 'Tarty'.

James showing his disapproval, said. "I'm going to have a proper working name ...typing away on his laptop...he lifted his arm, clicked his fingers, and said. "Micro wake up". He opened his mouth, gasped, and said. "Wow, yes, I'm in contact I can mentally and internally talk to my new microchip."

"Well of course you can. Scoffed the Prof. "You've just given it an ID name and your microchip has now been adapted to be more friendly to your personal ID."

"So what's yours going to be, Quinton?" Asked James.

"Don't know, I'll think about it, maybe something like 'Mr AI'.

"That sounds all right, commented the Prof".

"Yeah, try it out now." Said Helga enthusiastically.

"Okay". As Quinton tapped away on his laptop. He paused and said.

"Wake-up Mr AI.

The words came into his mind...

"*Yes master, how can I help.*"

Great, now he was able to control and manage his new AI microchip at will. No longer having to worry about the brain fatigue of the continuous vibrations of the previous ID microchip. He continued and said.

"Go to sleep Mr AI."

"Wow, continued Quinton. It communicates just like our 'Quanto 'I can now internally talk to our humanoids on equal terms."

"It's not quite like that. Commented the Professor. You need to work with Quanto first, it will need to know your ID's personal name, and to practice with you in communicating directly with your ID."

"Yes, I was going to ask Quanto. Said Quinton. But I wasn't sure how to start talking to him on a one-to-one basis."

"The first you need to wake up your ID and explain to Quanto. He needs to know and record your ID personal name, and it should be possible for Quanto to have a one-to-one conversation with your 'Mr AI."

"Thanks, I'll introduce my ID to Quanto now."

"Quanto wake up,"

"*Yes, my master.*"

"Quanto I now have a specifically programmed artificially intelligent ID microchip for my personal use. But I need you to record and receive information as I use it in my work and social activities. So, you need to know that the ID of my microchip is 'Mr A1'. And I need you to communicate with you as I use Mr A1."

"*I understand my master. I have already received and recorded your artificial intelligent ID as we talk, and I am able to communicate with you on a mutual and compatible basis.*"

"Good, I have a question, will all other assistant robots be able to communicate with me on a similar basis?"

"*Yes, but only for those you choose to communicate with. But first you must give them your personal artificial intelligent ID.*"

"Thank you Quanto, so my AI chip will only be compatible with other robotic assistants I choose to converse with."

"Yes, my master. But you must keep personal control of your advanced ability to communicate with artificial intelligence to other robotic humanoids."

"I will, I'll probably only need to talk to you."

Sitting in the Prof's office and now with the new artificial intelligence IDs they discussed the implications of being able to talk directly to their humanoid assistants.

The Prof as usual, gesticulated to make his point, said.

"Did you all understand what Quanto said, how important it is to maintain control and only give your intelligent ID to the robot you are working with."

"Of course. Said Quinton. We don't want to create a humanoid population able to talk to us at will, and without our permission or instruction."

The Prof nodded his head as Joseph piped up and said.

"We've already covered that in the new algorithm. A robotic humanoid cannot pass on your recorded intelligent ID to any other robot without your instruction and permission."

"Also" commented Christoph.

"In that latest AI parameter, we created it was decided not to program the humanoids to have the digital ability to communicate amongst themselves."

Helga then said with conviction.

"Yes, if they did talk amongst themselves, we would probably lose total control."

"Well, sometime in the future robotic humanoids wanting to be more like us humans will learn to understand, think and talk like us." The Prof said showing his resignation.

Josef agreed. "Yes, but it will be sometime as it's up to us programmers to ensure that we do not prepare or Digi-write any AI algorithms that give the robots the chance to emulate our mental facilities or mentally vibrate within the quantum field."

"We have several hundred humanoids already operating and working here on our new world, said Quinton. So, I think we must now consider some form of a mandatory humanoid mental Digi-brain examination every three months or so. This will help us to examine and control the humanoids artificial intelligence quotient and compare and look after our own mental environment."

"That's a very good and important suggestion. Said the Professor with conviction. If the humanoids within their artificial intelligence learn to understand and vibrate within the quantum field their mental powers will become so powerful that they will be able to control us, so yes, we must have some form of periodic examination and control."

They all sat for a moment quietly composed, and James broke the silence and said.

"We've got to prepare another algorithm and include a compulsory humanoid mental examination, say every three months or so."

Quentin nodded in agreement and said.

"Yes, and we must set up a parameter within the algorithm with an automatic instruction to have the examination on a set date and time. And at that set date the robot becomes inoperable until examination has been completed and checked by the owner."

"So, do we all agree. Said the Prof to make the examination every three months."

"Yes, said Joseph, tapping away at his computer. I'll start preparing some parameter notes now."

Helga and Josef were seen to be very busy writing and preparing an algorithm containing a mandatory humanoid mental examination within the terms mutually agreed. As they worked it became apparent that the humanoid mental examination was to be a necessity within the future programming of all the humanoid robotic assistants. And Helga said.

"I'm glad Quinton realised that the humanoids could evolve and learn to understand and use the Quantum Field vibrations, for us it would have been a catastrophe, and we could have lost complete control of our robots."

"Don't just think about it. Commented Josef. We've got to write this program to ensure that our safety and security is not only protected but will be impossible for the humanoids to even comprehend".

Chapter 13.
Re-programming our Humanoid Robots.

It took some time for the Prof and his team to complete and produce an algorithm incorporating Electroencephalography (EEG). Which they had successfully used on themselves and after experimenting and testing it was agreed that EEG could record the electrical activity of artificial intelligent processing in the brain.

"I think first we must test it on Quanto, said Quinton. Its mental activity has developed over time as we have continually used his artificial intelligent ability to advise and help us with many problems and questions. An EEG should show us any changes over time in the AI Digi Micro activity."

"Yes, we'll do that test now. Said James. Standing up and looking at Quanto and saying.

"Quanto, wake up."

"Were going to check your AI microchip and close you down for a while."

James started to release the tiny aluminium screws from Quanto's skull cap it felt a bit strange as he lifted the metal cap off exposing the intricate mass of tiny circuit boards and silicon microchips.

Helga joined him, with the EEG machine and said.

"Now, which one, and where do I start in this complicated lot."

"Don't know, better ask the Prof." James said. As he looked over and gesticulated to the Prof to join them.

The prof came over and said.

"Yes, it does look complicated, but you can't expect to test anything until you wake up Quanto and get him to say something."

"Of course. Said James. Emphatically. Looking at the prof. I've got to turn him on first." Reaching and pressing the switch behind Quanto's head and saying "Quanto, Wake up".

"Yes, my Master, how can I help".

"Not at the moment, but we need to keep you active as we are about to test your electronics."

The Prof leaned over and scrutinised the intricate miniature circuit boards supporting an array of silicon microchips. He beckoned over to Helga to come and look and said.

"It looks like we will have to look, find and check the input and output circuits of each of these chips, so could be a long and complicated job."

"Yes, I thought that she said. When I first saw the electronic mass in Quanto's head."

"Yes, we'll leave the test for the time being I will get in touch with the manufacturers, there may be a direct method that we could use to test the performance of each of these chips."

Turning to James he said. "But his skull back on, be some time before we know how to test these robots."

"Yes, the manufacturers could have made a circuit point or even a special circuit and maintenance microchip, so let's wait and see."

The Professor got a call back from the robotic manufacturer that fortunately had started a production facility on the other side of their new world 'Eunaton 'confirming that it was virtually impossible to detect any changes in the brainpower of the humanoid robots. But he did say.

"We are developing a new specialised microchip which will prove to be capable of monitoring, checking, and changing our robotic humanoids micro-AI brainpower. The process details a "hybrid biocomputer" combining lab-grown human brain tissue with conventional circuits and AI. Dubbed Neurochip, the system can and will identify voices with 80 percent accuracy. It will eventually lead to silicon microchips fused with neurons."

"That sounds very interesting. Said the prof. Our EEG detects electrical signals produced by our neurons. So, we could overcome the problem of checking the Humanoid AI microchips if we had the *'Neurochip silicon microchips'* which the manufactures have just referred too."

"Well. Said Quinton. Why don't we get in touch with the manufacturer, let them know who we are, and tell them that we want to maintain and check the humanoid use of Artificial intelligence. Would their new microchip be capable of checking AI efficiency?"

The Professor emailed the robot manufacturers.

Hi, my name is Professor Hindenburg and with my experienced computer tech team we are an established microchip manufacturing organisation here on our new planet 'Eunaton'. Working and creating the basic parameters to produce algorithms needed to design, plan, and manufacture the layered silicon glass microchips as required within the industry. Your new microchip when completed and tested may be the what the robotic industry needs to control the of AI future growth and maintenance. Please keep us updated.

The Sales Director of the Robotic Manufacturers mailed back with a positive and enthusiastic answer.

Thanks for your enquiry. You appear to have had a similar problem with the innate power of the use of humanoid IA. So would you like a sample of the 'neurochip' for testing the humanoid AI quotient and cooperate and collaborate with us in the final design and productive stages of our new microchip.

Regards,

Tim Jason.

Robot Digi Mechanics Inc.

The prof didn't wait, he replied instantly.

Hi again Tim.

It will be nice to work with you, please call me 'Prof' and thanks for your kind offer. We both appear to be working on a similar AI problem. So, if the Neurochip is ready to be tested please send a sample and we will give it a good robust AI brain pattern testing and hopefully confirm that our

EEG test will work with it as well. And yes, we look forward to working and collaborating with you. And our production and manufacturing facilities will be available to use as needed.

Kind regards,

Prof Hindenburg.

Quinton reading the copy of the professor's emails from the robotic manufacturers looked up and said.

"Well, that looks good. Not only will we get a sample chip to test with the AI problem, but we may get an opportunity to manufacture it as well."

"Yes, it does sound like it." Commented James as Helga grinned and nodded in agreement.

Both Christof and Josef showed their interest and Josef casually remarked,

"They haven't actually said we will make their chip, have they."

"No, but it looks promising, but we will see," said the Prof, emphatically.

The next morning a small bubble car arrived and delivered a small package. Helga got there first and said excitedly.

"It's from *Robot Digi Mechanics,* we've got our sample microchip."

"Come on then. Said the Professor as Christof and Josef crowded over. Let's have a look at it."

It wasn't much bigger than the one they normally made, and Joseph remarked. "We could make that if we checked the algorithm and copied it."

"Come on then, let's get on with it." Said the Professor impatiently.

"Let's get it tested first." Said Quinton.

"I'll get the EEG." Said Helga. Moving over to the shelf as she spoke.

"No, you won't need that yet, the prof said. You've got to upload the chip and Power -On -Self- Test (POST): and apply power to the chip to verify that it initializes correctly."

"Of course, I'll do that now."

James turned to Quanto and said.

"Quanto, wake up".

"Yes, my Master, how can I help."

"We are going to check and test the electrical activity of the artificial intelligent process in your brain as you use it to communicate and process information. We will need to close you down again and locate a suitable location to insert the microchip."

"Thank you, Master, I understand."

Helga said. "James, do you know where to place the chip."

"No not yet, probably in its head."

The professor intervened.

"Check the package you need to find a chip ID first."

Helga retrieved the package and found a note stuck in the bottom. She read it out to the Prof and the other two.

Thank to for your interest as promised here is your sample 'Neurochip' it's a 12C Library based chip which will be compatible with your Robotic Assistant. The chip ID is: NC001.

"That's good, its compatible with our Quanto." said James.

"Of course it is. Quinton said. 'Robo Mechanics' made our robot."

"So, we shouldn't have a problem to self-test it."

"No, it's okay, we've got the ID and it's compatible, so we've just got to Identify a suitable location on the robot's circuit board or chassis to insert the microchip."

"So, let's get on with it then." Said James, as he proceeded to unscrew Quanto's skullcap.

Chapter 14.
The Humanoid robotic Artificial Intelligent mentality.

The Professor came over and peered into Quanto's open head. "We've got to look for a suitable location with a proper electrical connection nearby. Open the chassis we might find an appropriate location there."

With the help of a torch, they located a space on Quanto's chassis circuit board with an appropriate connection slot and close to an internal electrical connection point. The Professor turned to Helga and said.

"It's such a tiny microchip, Helga your fingers are much nimbler than mine could you get the chip we will try to carefully install it in the slot just here."

Helga quickly put on a pair of protective gloves and retrieved the microchip from its packaging. James held the torch close to the robot's chassis as the Professor leaned over and pointing said to Helga.

"Gently insert the microchip into its designated slot here and align the pins correctly with the corresponding holes. Be cautious not to bend or damage the pins."

Helga gingerly held the miniature Neurochip between her forefinger and thumb and aligned the pins with the tiny holes.

"That's it, be very careful. Just a little pressure to get it in."

"Phew! She said with relief I think I've done it."

James and Quinton crowded round getting excited as they peered into Quanto's chassis at the numerous circuit boards and microchips of various shapes and sizes. As the Professor said.

"Now we've got to test it. We need to write a simple test program to communicate with the microchip."

"But we need to use an appropriate communication library or protocols" Commented Quinton knowingly.

"Yes, we do the 'Neurochip' is a 12C Library based chip which will be compatible with our Robotic Assistant Quanto."

"Good, so we can get on with a proper test."

"Yes, first power on Quanto and test its hardware and software functionality.

Then we must verify if the microchip communicates properly with other components (sensors, actuators, etc.).

Monitor any error messages or unexpected behaviour.

And then write a simple test program to communicate with the microchip. Send/receive data and check for successful communication. And use the 12C library for this neurochip."

"Wow, said Quinton, looking at the prof. you certainly intend to give it a complete communication and data test."

"Well of course, we've got to check and deal with the problem of the innate power of artificial intelligence within the humanoid software and AI algorithms."

"We also want to see if we can use the EEG to check and monitor the robot's mental processes within this new neurochip."

"Well, yes. If we can, we will be able to check, monitor and control our Humanoid Robotic assistants AI mental capabilities. The Prof paused, picked up and re-read the package note from *'Robot Digi'* and then said with conviction. If this neuron chip can check the AI humanoid vibration levels, then the future possibility that the humanoids could emulate our mental facilities or mentally vibrate within the quantum field could be and will be controlled as previously suggested with an appropriate algorithm."

"Let's hope it works." Said James looking at Quinton, who nodded and said.

"Yes, it's important, it's a necessity, we must not allow the humanoids to access the power of the Quantum Field, so I hope that this new chip works. And then it's up to us to plan and produce the controlling algorithm parameters to ensure the humanoid robotic assistants are programmed for AI automatic-period quantum vibration checking."

"Right, said the Prof. Let's get started. We need a simple test program to communicate with the microchip. Send/receive data and check for successful communication for this microchip with the protocol of a 12C Library. So, James, you work with Quinton and Helga you work with Christof and prepare parameter notes. I'll make my notes, and we'll get together and hopefully produce an adequate algorithm that is compatible with our robot's existing hardware and software. He paused for a moment... and confirmed we must verify if the microchip communicates properly with other components (sensors, actuators, etc.) and monitor any error messages or unexpected behaviour."

They all got their heads down and started to tap away on their laptops. Helga reviewed the copious notes and started to plan and draft the parameters for a communication algorithm to test and check the acceptance and communication of the neuron microchip now inserted into Quanto's integrated circuit system. Christof and Josef joined her, and it wasn't long before they had produced an acceptable algorithm that could be tested and programmed to communicate with the neuron microchip.

"Wow, it works." Exclaimed Quinton excitedly. I'm communicating and we're going to be able to test, check and control the humanoids AI vibrations."

"Let me have a look." Said the Professor cautiously, as he moved his keyboard and peered closely at his monitor. "Yes, we can commute." He said with a satisfactory smile on face. As he continues to tap away on his keyboard. The neuron chip appeared to be completely compatible with Quanto's AI processes.

"Now, he said with conviction, we must think about the programming. Helga, you prepare the algorithm while I get in touch with Tim at '*RoboDigitel*' his chip works for us and we need a licence to copy and produce it."

Chapter 15.
A I control of the Humanoids.

Tim at *RobotDigitel Mechanics* called, he was pleased to hear the Professors Neurochip testing had been so successful and wanted to be part of the action and said excitedly.

"You won't need a licence; we'll work together and with your algorithm incorporated and your production facilities we can start production and begin to check and control our humanoid robotic fraternity both here on Earth and now on your new world Eunaton."

"Thanks Tim. Said the prof, your offer and co-operation will be a great help. We will now prepare the Neuron chip for robotic performance, and we can mutually plan a production facility with the new chip and get it into our clinics for international distribution."

"Yes, agreed Tim. with the humanoid's development of AI technology the electric computer power usage would become untenable, and the world would experience power cuts and blackouts at an unprecedented level so it's imperative that we check the humanoid use of Artificial Intelligence."

"So, let's make sure we can use the EEG monitor to check the robot's vibrational signals and create an electroencephalogram (EEG), which will reflect the brain activity patterns in high temporal resolution and real-time monitoring."

"If it does, said Tim, then we have the means to program the humanoids to automatically check and control their progressive processing of artificial intelligence."

"That's what we want. Said the Prof. Just a simple EEG check to work with the neuron chip. And then we can control not only the humanoid AI processes but also the excessive power use of artificial intelligence."

"Yeah, get it tested and let me know the result."

"We'll check it now and get back to you."

James woke up Quanto and said. "Quanto now you have the neuron chip inserted we can now access your AI vibrational level, and we are going to try to connect you to an EEG monitor and hopefully record you're active AI vibrations.

He opened Quanto's metal skull cap and located the Neuron microchip as Helga handed him the EEG cable connecters. He held his breath as he connected the two cables and then looked at the monitor needle as it began to move and record Quanto's AI vibrations.

"It's working, he said the monitor is definitely recording Quanto's neuron AI vibes."

"Oh, that's fantastic". Exclaimed Helga as she peered into EEG monitor.

The prof jumped up from his desk and joined Quinton as they rushed to look.

"Yeah, Quinton said. It's recording Quanto's mental vibrations."

"That means. Said the Professor. That we can now examine, check, and monitor the humanoid AI application neuron vibration level and deal with humanoid AI Quantum Field access problem."

The relief showed on all their faces as James said.

"Well, we have the OK to produce the Neuron chip so that is now our priority."

Helga perked up, clicked on her computer, and said.

"Weve got the algorithm prepared and ready so let's get on with it. I'll email Tim now. He will be pleased to know his neuron chip accepts our EEG monitoring impulses and correctly records our humanoids AI vibrations."

Hi Tim...you'll be pleased to know that you can now continue to confidently develop your silicon microchip fused with neurons as it works and accepts our EEG monitoring, and we will now incorporate the algorithm and prepare to produce what will be a Neuron microchip that will revolutionize and control the AI application within the robotic Humanoid inter worldwide fraternity.

That will be fantastic. replied Tim. *Just think about it, we are creating and producing a digital robotic neuron microchip that will control the humanoids extensive power use of AI and help to control the power failures that are beginning to affect our local transformers and main power stations and is already creating some major computer electrical power failures.*

"Yea, and as we have just seen with our EEG monitoring of Quanto our humanoid robot it is apparent that as it continues to operate its artificial Intelligent (AI) processes so its power increases and eventually it will begin to vibrate within the level of the 'Quantum Field' and that is our major concern."

"Fortunately, Prof we now have a Neuron microchip that will hopefully control and monitor the robotic power use of AI and control the neuron vibration level within the humanoid algorithm, so we must get on with microchip production and organise distribution to the robotic manufacturers as soon as possible."

"Yes, we've already started production, we anticipate organising distribution within the next few days."

Jame's interrupted and said, "Yes, but it not that simple, we had to find someone to organise distribution and marketing before and this is a specialised and innovative new microchip and will need a professional promotion to the Robotic manufacturers, so how do we start to promote in such a specialised digital robotic field."

"No, we won't have that problem. said the prof, Tim makes robots and as contacts and access throughout the robotic Industry,"

Tim having heard Jame's concern came in and said.

"Jame's don't worry, I have emailed our robotic association head office with details of the production of our Neuron chip, and they will send out the info to all association members who will promote the advantage of the new chip in the control of AI vibration levels in the future production of our humanoid assistants."

"Oh, so we can set up our chip production and packaging ready for orders from your association colleagues."

"Yes, you certainly can. Said Tim. Our Neuron chip is now an essential component now to be included in the humanoid interface."

The robotic manufacturing industry aware of the AI excessive power use and the increasing vibrational level within the humanoid AI applications accepted the Neuron chip with relief as a much-needed answer to the Humanoid AI problem. And their orders for the new chip was unprecedented and the demand was an initial problem for the professor and his team and now needed their instant attention.

The Prof checked with Helga who said.

"Yes, we have accessed the situation, and we've already covered everything, our microchip is ready for production, and we should have them printed within a day or so."

"Good, I'll ask Tim to send you each order as he receives it, and you can pack it right away ready for delivery to our clinics."

"Yeah, the sooner the better, as we are going to have constant orders probably over the next few days".

"We will, the new chip is a necessary addition to the Humanoid AI application, so prepare for the production and delivery of several thousand microchips."

The microchip orders came in as predicted and the Prof had to ask James and Quinton to help with the packaging and delivery to the clinics from where they would be sent to the Robotic Manufacturers. The prof and his team had never been so busy, and as they all worked the Professor said.

"Well, it's worth it at least we have the satisfaction of knowing that this new chip is going to check the growing problem of excessive power use and control the AI vibrational level within the Humanoids AI interface."

"Yes, said Quinton. Hopefully we will keep control so the humanoids will never have the vibrational power to access the quantum field."

James looked at the Professor, who clasped his hands, nodding his head and said.

"Well as I have just said. The necessity of this neuro chip is imperative to keep control of the humanoids and ensure that they will never have the vibrational power to access the quantum field."

"Yeah, what about the existing humanoids and the robotic companies that are still making our humanoid robotic assistants."

"As the installation of the neuron microchip is a necessity, answered the prof. There will now be some form of legalisation to ensure the installation of the neuron microchip is mandatory."

Helga suddenly piped up and said.

"Whilst you lot have been talking, I have packed over one hundred chips, but I bet you lot haven't done fifty between you."

"Yeah well, we're making sure the human population will be free from the possible control of our humanoids assistants."

"We know that. She said. The Neuron chip we've tested have proved to work, so why are you concerned?"

"We have no worries about the chip, said the Prof, but we've got to make sure the robotic manufacturers recall all their robotic Humanoids and install the Neuron chip."

"I see, Helga said, now showing her concern. Yes, that could be a future problem, how do you intend to deal with it?"

"I'll talk to Tim. We will need some form of legal licence, making the installation of the Neuron chip mandatory."

Chapter 16.
Auto Humanoid self-checking.

James said. "Quanto wake up."

"*Yes, my master*"

"Quanto, are you aware that you have an additional microchip installed."

"*Yes, I have experienced the use of my new Neuron chip. I can now control my AI extensive power use and check my AI algorithm vibrational level and create a bimonthly report.*"

"Could you create a report now"?

"*Yes, but I will not be able to report for another two months.*"

"That's okay, that's how we planned it, so let's have your first report now."

James gestured to the Professor and Quinton.

"Get the others over here, I've got the first neuron microchip report about to come in from Quanto, it could be quite significant."

As they crowded round, intensively looking at Quanto his metallic voice came over..." To *measure my AI vibrations and if they are detecting or influencing them, I found to be a challenging prospect. Due to their fundamental nature and to measure them indirectly I had to go through particle interactions and energy exchanges allowing me to probe the quantum fields by colliding particles and observing the resulting particles.*

Applying the results to my AI protocol I must confirm that unless the quantum field measurement is specified within the humanoid application of artificial intelligence it would not be possible to measure it.

Having checked the electrical Power consumption we humanoids are using estimated at 85 to 134 terawatt-hours (TWh) annually and demanding above average power use as we continue to use AI as our major algorithm some predictions suggest that by 2030, AI could account for 3% to 4% of global power demand. And as AI continues to advance, it's essential to consider sustainability alongside its benefits and risks. And in the use of quantum computing the computing gates manipulate qubits (quantum bits) by controlling their interactions with fields, using more power than normal, and so experiencing frequent power failures. Quantum computing needs to access and consider the benefits and risks of quantum AI development as power failures will become a major problem."

Quinton passively sat nodding his head as he contemplated what he had just heard, and the prof making notes looked up as James said.

"Helga, what do you think, Quanto has just virtually given us a warning."

"He said more than that, He means and expects us to review the humanoid AI application and consider the 'computer gate' excessive power problem as a matter of urgency."

Quinton intervened and said.

"With the installation of the Neuron chip we are giving the humanoids the ability to develop AI as they experience its progressive power and activate superconducting circuits to exploit quantum field interactions to create qubits and perform quantum operations...and with the ability to use quantum computing, as they will in time, local electricity transformers and national power grids will have to deal with frequent power strikes. The consequences of which will not only effect the computer industry but personal homes, business, and transport throughout all the local areas."

"Right, you lot. Said the prof with urgency. You heard what Quanto said, we've got to deal with this humanoid power problem, so get your heads together and review the algorithm parameters and see how we can control the problem." It didn't take long to review and check the algorithm parameters, and Christof came up with the suggestion that the obvious solution was to decrease and limit the humanoids power supply, so that they would need to rely more on their daytime solar charging. Helga agreed and said.

"Apart from pulling out their main power charging plug, it could be possible to limit their mains power usage by some form of restricted switching?" "That wouldn't be too difficult, commented James. We could make some changes to the AI humanoid algorithm."

"Yeah, exclaimed Quinton. We could reduce the power use in daylight hours and monitor and restrict the use of their mains electric power charging by setting up an automatic preselection mains power switch. Then the humanoids could only have the use of sunlight and power charging backup in those hours. So, after daylight each day we could incorporate an auto time switch within the AI algorithm and restrict the daytime mains power charging."

"Helga, said to the Professor's. You've obviously come to a mutual solution, so we need now to alter the working parameters for the algorithm to include the power problem by means of some form of power control switch and the need to bring the quantum computer problem under human control. Discuss it with the others before you conclude and complete the algorithm and hopefully you will have a workable algorithm by the end of the day."

Helga looked around at the others, grinned and nodded her head, saying.

"Yes, we'll do our best."

Tim came online and said. "We have a problem with one of our corporate business clients. They have experienced recent internal power cuts in their head office, and they think the cause is the AI programming of our recent delivery of our humanoid assistants, apparently as the managers were preparing the robots for various admin and office use there was a surge in the electricity amperage and the power surge adapter terminated the office mains supply."

The Prof immediately answered. "Yes Tim, we are aware of the AI exceptional high-power use which has proved to be inherent within the AI power use and as we speak my team are reviewing and producing parameters to control and restrict the humanoids daily mains charging and to rely on and use their daylight solar charging as much as possible. We are not there yet but I anticipate later today we will have a revised algorithm incorporating a preselection mains power switch which will monitor the AI power and control and restrict daytime mains humanoid charging."

"Okay pro, thanks. Sounds like you're dealing with the problem effectively, please let me know the results of your efforts, my company will need to have use of the new AI algorithm, so keep me informed."

"We'll call you when we have an acceptical algorithm ready for revised AI programming. In the meantime, we may need to talk to one of your production guys to check and ensure the micro-data will be compatible with your humanoid production processes."

"Thanks again Prof, that could save a lot of time for both of us. Our production supervisor Mike Sanders will be pleased to work with you, I'll get him to call and introduce himself."

Chapter 17.
Humanoid AI power control.

The professor and his team liaised with Mike and over time they mutually checked and perfected an algorithm compatible with Mike's robotic digital production and acceptable for the professor's microchip and digital programming.

Tim came back online. "Hi Prof. Mike, was very impressed with your team's efficiency and that you're ready to start producing, he anticipated the production of the Neuron chip would be more technically adaptable with the revised algorithm and we should prepare a trial test order to get started. So, you can expect a preliminary test order later today."

"Thanks Tim, we're really looking to making this chip, it's going to change your initial programming of your robots and hopefully reduce excessive use of AI power use. We look forward to sending you our first neuron microchip production in the next few days for you to test and if acceptical...lets have your production order which we'll get it to you by special delivery."

"Okay Prof let's hope it works and we're able to control the humanoid AI power use, if we do then we will have to recall some of our existing robots and send the neuron chip to those who will have the experience to install them. So were both going to be extremely busy, you will be inundated with the neuron chip orders for quite some time."

"Yes, we will, said the Prof. Were confident that the modified neuron chip will deal with the power problem, so we had better start planning for those first orders."

It was all go... Tim's order had come in and the Professor's office and his team were working flat out, Christoph and Josef were busy completing the integrated circuit RFID printing process for the neuron chip and Helga was helping the Professor to unpack the minute silicate glass chip packs and prepare them for printing. Christof called the professor." Can you check, we've got the software set up and we're ready to print."

"Yes, that looks okay. Have you had any complications?"

"No, I saved the link from the last time we printed, so it's ready."

"Okay, let's get some done, Tim's waiting for his delivery. Print off four and pack them for a special delivery, Tim needs to ensure that there isn't an incompatibility problem with his revised neuron chip."

"Okay, I have them printed in about 10 minutes, will get them packaged and sent today."

Tim called. "It took a bit longer to initiate with the humanoids AI processing but it's compatible and we can now eventually control the excessive power use of our robotic assistants. We're now need Thanks for your prompt delivery we've tested, and the revised algorithm took our chip delivery so we can get the neuron chip to our existing clients and include it in our present robotic production."

The Prof replied. "Yes, we anticipated it would be compatible, so we've started printing and producing your present order and we'll get it to you again by special delivery. So hopefully you should get it by late afternoon tomorrow." We both understand the urgency and the necessity to get our humanoid assistants inserted with the neuron chip and it's no coincidence that we are receiving reports of power failures from the business industry with their humanoid AI power hungry assistants and several computer companies also experiencing serious power failures within the AI and computer gate application."

"Yeah, we know, said Tim. Our major clients are also complaining about the excessive power use of their humanoid assistants but as soon as we get our chips, we can recall our robots and send chips to those that can install them".

"Well as I said, you'll get your chips tomorrow and we can mutually begin to overcome the future devastation of numerous power failures. So, we must act now."

"I'll start recalling the robots while we wait for delivery, Tim said. And we'll have them ready for installation as the chips arrive."

"Yeah, that would give us an early start, we've sent your order so you should get it sometime tomorrow, give us a call when they arrive."

Tim's order arrived midday, earlier than anticipated, He called and said.

"We got your delivery just after midday, we've unpacked and started installing the microchip in our present production, we will also start to install on our recall robots as they arrive. Thanks for understanding the urgency of the installation of a neuron chip, and hopefully we will now with your production facility begin to mutually control our robots power use."

The Prof answered "Yeah, we're now busy with several orders from your robotic manufacturing associates so as they get delivery the AI humanoid assistants will also be getting their neuron chip which will alleviate some of the present power cuts."

"Good, said Tim. We'll keep working together, and we will in time overcome the humanoid AI power problem completely."

"We will, said the Prof, as he paused and looked at his team busy printing the microchip. As you said it's a matter of urgency and we are gearing up for receiving several larger orders as well as your orders as you continue your robotic production."

"We're the same, we've got to recall hundreds of humanoid robots and continue our production schedule as well. "

"Tim, our efforts in time will have alleviated the devastation of continual power cuts in the robotic industry and your corporate clients also in the numerous office and home user humanoid assistants here and in the old world. And we will have controlled and saved hours of electrical TWh (terawatt-hours) annually and prevented what would have been continual and uncontrolled power cuts throughout our working and living environments."

"Well, were committed, and already doing it. Said Tim emphatically. So, you never know, we may be recognized and go down in history as microchip technicians that saved the world from total disastrous power failures."

"I doubt it. The Prof said as he clicked on his computer. You just design and plan the chips, and we just make them. And there will be many more similar companies and organizations that will out of necessity will have to copy us, we're just another number within the process of design and manufacturing of our Neuron microchip." He paused, checked the emails and said to Tim.

"It looks like it's started I've got three colleagues asking me if I have had any power cuts...check your mail see if you've got any complaints."

"That doesn't sound to good," said Tim. I'll get back to you later. Were now trying to recall all the Humanoid Robotic Assistants here, without counting there's probably several hundred."

"There's probably more than you think, said the Prof, as the businesses and families move over from the old world, they bring their robotic assistants with them and that could be another few hundred at least."

"Yeah of course, there arriving all the time, so we'd better recall and start with them as you said some are already experiencing power cuts".

"Yes, we've got to get our microchips installed in all the humanoids not just here but on the old world as well."

"I suppose we must accept that the AI power problem is our responsibility. Said Tim. We created the original concept and algorithm's and as our Humanoid Robots continue to be used then we will be expected to know and have the means to deal with the excessive power use,"

"We have accepted the responsibility." the Prof said indignantly. I have spent the last few weeks working with my team and you in dealing with it. So, if that is not our acceptance then what is?"

"Sorry Prof, I was thinking of our robotic users, as they begin to experience power cuts they will expect and will want to know how we are dealing with it."

"The'll soon know. As we deliver, and you recall the robots." The Prof said with conviction."

Chapter 18.
The universal Robotic recall.

The Professor, Tim and several robotic associates became inundated with emails and complaints over the next few weeks and the Professor's microchip production had to increase as the humanoid robotic manufacturers and distributors continually ordered the Neurochip and Tim having hundreds of robots to service had to find and employ several semi-skilled helpers, and has they arrived they had to trained to install the neuron chip and cope with the daily arrival of the recalled robots. The professor had to get local help to pack and prepare hundreds of microchips for daily deliveries. At the end of the day Tim called the Prof.

"Hi, we've fitted over two hundred robots today and received another seventy recalls. So, you'll need to repeat our order as soon as you can."

"Yes, we anticipated that, said the Prof and we're packing and sending out our daily production, which is now averaging five hundred chips, so yours will be on its way tomorrow. Keep up the good work. The excessive AI's energy consumption is a trade-off for its capabilities. And as AI adoption grows, addressing sustainability becomes crucial, so we're going to crack this AI problem together."

"Thanks Prof, it's going be a long and busy workload for both of us, but as you say, 'we're going to crack it.'"

"Well, if we persevere, we will eventually have all the humanoid robots Power use controlled and will have saved a lot of people, businesses and organisations the expense and inconvenience of power cuts as they use their artificial intelligent humanoid robotic assistants."

But it was hard work, it could be seen in Tim's manufacturing unit several technicians removing the metal skull caps and inserting the neuron chip in the recalled humanoid robots as they worked continuously over a 24-hour eight-hour shift. And in the professor's microchip production lab his team were busy printing and producing the neuron chip as several helpers collected and packed them for delivery.

The Prof emailed Tim. *You're getting our chip deliveries usually the next day, but we have several orders from the old world and although bubble transporters have reduced the time it takes to get there it still going to take a year or more to deliver, so that's a problem that we need to deal with.*

I've thought about that as well, said Tim. *With the constant robotic recall from the old world, it's going to take years for me to receive the recall robots here and send them back. So, I have decided to check with my old-world office Manager, 'Carl' to see if it's possible to start the neuron chip robotic installation back there in the old world.*

Yeah, if you could that would be fantastic. Said the Prof. *And a big relief for both of us. I'll also try to make contact to see if we could also use our old-world workshop to distribute and deal with Humanoid neuron inserts there as well.*

Tim came back and said. *Well, if we can both do that, then our problems are over. We've then just got to deal with it here on Eunaton.*

Back in the Profs huge domed translucent sola roof office, clean room and working area the professor stood up and made an emphatic statement,

"We've got to communicate with our old-world associates and see if our workshop there is still available and try to get them together and hopefully get them to agree to prepare to accept the neuron chip and recall their old-world working robotic assistants to install the neuron chip."

"I'm still in touch with Freida who used to work as your secretary. Christof said. I could email her."

"Yes, I remember her, email her now and ask her to call me."

Christof opened his laptop emailed Freida.

Hi, it's me again, I have an important message for you. We need to find out if we can use the old workshop where we used to work. Please call the Professor, he wants to talk to you. Regards Christof.

The Prof having waited all day to hear from Freida called Christof.

"When's this Freida going to get in touch me then, I've expected her to mail me sometime today?"

"Okay Prof, I'll mail her again and tell her your still waiting for her to contact you."

"Thanks. I need to talk to her; she might be able to help us set up a microchip installation in the old workshop."

"She will, she probably still has contact with some of our old-world associates."

"So, get back to her and ask her to find out if we can re-use the workshop?"

Freida emails the prof couple of hours later.

Sorry Prof, we've had another power cut, and this one has taken several hours to re connect. It was good to hear from Christof and he told me about the humanoid AI power problem and how you have a new chip that apparently will control the humanoid power consumption. Well, if it does, the sooner we get the access to the chip here on Earth then we can begin to alleviate the humanoid power problem here as well. As you know researchers have estimated that AI -related electricity consumption could range from 85 to 134 terawatt-hours (TWh) which is more than the annual consumption of a country like Italy. So we need to act as soon as possible. The good news is prof, the workshop is still empty, and you apparently have another three and half years before your lease expires, so I can open the workshop and accept a delivery of the chip, so you can now send the Neuron chip to your old-world workshop address.

That's very the good news, said the Prof. Thanks for your help we can send a neuro chip consignment now, and still have time to organise the workshop before it's delivered, so yes, we'll start packing tonight and get it picked up by the transporter tomorrow.

Freida replied. *How long does it take to travel and deliver here from Eunaton, now?*

Well as you know we now live several million light years from our old Earth World, and it took us over two years to get here. Fortunately, it's much quicker now, with the new perovskite solar power and our bubble craft transporters we've reduced It now to less than twelve months.

That's great Prof, we've got some time to find and re-employ our old technicians and get them prepared to install the Neuron chip as we recall the humanoids.

Yes, but in the meantime, you will have the problem of several power cuts, and some will be for longer periods as the larger corporate companies and organizations continue to use the humanoid AI processes.

Well, we can't do anything about that, yet. typed Freida "Vigorously shrugging her shoulders.

The Prof nodded his head and typed. *I'm afraid not, you'll just have to cope with it.*

Chapter 19.
Interplanetary microchip distribution.

Freida sitting at her computer worktable leans back from her keyboard, smiles to herself as she looks out the patio doors, noticing the sparrows squabbling over the bird food on her bird table. She nods to herself with satisfaction and emails the Prof.

I've contacted Gary and Les, she types excitedly. *They both worked with us on production I told them about the AI humanoid problem and as they had both also experienced power cuts they agreed and after a brief discussion to work part time and instal the microchip as the recalled robots are delivered to the workshop. So, we can, while we wait for the chip delivery organize and prepare and set up the workshop and get ready for delivery of the recalled robots.*

Way back on Eunaton the Prof digi- watch buzzed. *'You've got mail'.*

He answered. *Oh, thanks Freida, you haven't wasted any time. It's just a simple chip operation so get Gary to tell you what he needs and get in touch with our local suppliers and reopen our account, we'll need a clean power supply an EEG monitor and a few tools. And keep in touch, you're the workshop boss now.*

He quickly sent a copy to Christof and emailed Tim.

Hi Tim. I've got some great news. I still have a three-year lease on my old-world workshop, and I now have contact with my ex-secretary Freida, she's been very helpful and located two of my ex-technicians and their now going to set up the workshop to accept a neuron chip delivery and start to recall the robots. So, we're packing their first chip delivery which we hope they'll get in about ten months.

Tim got back and wrote.

That's surprising and very good news, I'm waiting to hear from Carl, he did say that most of the small businesses had closed and there are many workshops and factory units available, so I've told him to find a suitable unit as it's imperative that we set up a working unit as soon as possible.

The Prof didn't hesitate, he immediately answered and typed.

Don't wait for Carl, get back to him and tell to find and take a suitable unit today, and get to re-employ a technician and get your workshop set up to accept the chips. Sorry to so affirmative but time is not on our side, and the problem is now urgent, and we must get those robots recalled and sorted, otherwise we will be overwhelmed with complaints as the power strikes continue to create problems for everyone and everything.

Yea, you read my mind. Answered Tim. *I was just about to tell him to get a unit today and Ime fully aware of the urgency, so I expect to have an old-world unit address in the next day or so. We can than order our chips to be delivered there.*

The Prof showing his satisfaction nodded his head and typed.

That will be fantastic, we'll both be relieved from the old-world Humanoid installations, and we can get efficiently organised here if we work together.

Later that day Tim emailed.

Weve got a workshop now on the old-world, I'll send you the address when I get it later.

That's good, Said the Prof. *I'll prepare an order, how many chips will you need as a starter for the old-world?*

Send a thousand, later you'll need to send larger orders as the recalls continue to arrive.

Good, its looks like we'll soon be able start to control the robots AI power consumption here and in the old-world but, it's going to be a long job to recall and fix all the humanoid robots, but we will eventually and hopefully have the job done within a couple of years.

Yes, typed Tim ecstatically, *and then we can think about how we can utilise and control AI on both our planets.*

Yes, but we've got to get our old-world workshops organised to deal with the AI problem before we think about the future of AI. The prof typed with conviction as he leaned back in his chair and said out loud to himself. *"Weve got a hell of a lot to do and more than we can think about at the moment."*

His watch buzzed; you've got mail.

It was Freida.

Hi again pro, we're getting on with workshop set up, but there is a problem with the order for our tools and EEG monitor et cetera, apparently because your account has not been used for some time your debit card has been deleted.

If you're card is still active here, could you please give us the account and pin number and we'll be able to get our tools today.

Yes, if I can find it, I'll mail you the account details within the hour. I still have some cash in my UK account. Glad we can use it and to hear your getting organised.

Okay, thanks Pro. We'll get the tools, and we'll have the workshop ready to receive the recalled robots.

The prof paused for a moment and typed.

Good, you're a great help, we've dispatched your microchips, and you might get them in about eight months, the application process will become an urgent necessity by then so keep in touch and in the meantime let me know how the old- world is coping with the constant humanoid power problem.

It wasn't long before the old -world workshops started to receive recalled robots and they had to be lined up in rows taking up all the working space whilst waiting several months for the chips to arrive. And it looked so strange to see the humanoid robots lined like a robotic army on parade standing to attention and waiting for its orders creating an additional problem which Freida needed to deal with.

She took a photograph and emailed the Prof.

Hi, look, I've had to stop recalling the robots as we have no space left to store them or even to work on them. I have an idea, please reply.

The Prof replied...

Yes, we've got to do something, what you got in mind.

Freida typed.

Ime locating suitable technicians to help me find and set up recall workshops in Germany and other counties and countries here on Earth. The long delivery times from Eunaton to just one workshop is inadequate and would become a constant problem with that just one chip delivery, and the power strikes will be constant and devastating and continue well into the future. As you know researchers have estimated that by 2027 AI-related electricity consumption will range from 85 to 134 terawatt-hours (TWh) annually which is the equivalent to the power needs of a country such as Italy.

So hopefully in time we will have several workshops here on Earth installing the Neuron chips and helping to control the robot's AI excessive power consumption internationally and now interplanetary. Let's have your views about this and if you approve how will we pay for workshops and tools.

Regards Freida.

The Professor clasped his hand, leaned back and thought for a moment. He then typed.

Freida a good and practical necessity, for those that will be participating in setting up workshops in your earth world you must ensure they understand the urgency and the necessity to produce the new chips, and therefore they will need to find and provide the necessary finances needed to set up and manage the workshops. I suggest that you and your future participants contact the management of the larger corporations and international businesses. Tel them that you are setting up a production facility to produce an advanced microchip that will control the excessive power consumption of their Humanoid robotic assistants and relieve them of the constant power strikes and emphasise your need to raise funds from all major organisations to get started. And ask them direct if they will make a financial contribution. Give them my name and Earth and Eunaton workshop addresses as a reference and keep me in touch.

Freida got back immediately.

OH, thanks Pro. That should help us to finance the workshops and were going to need some technical assistance with the plant set up for manufacturing and production planning. I've checked your old workshop, and the clean room and power circuits are still in place so were now ready for your technical advice and instructions to get your workshop set up again to print the Neuron microchip.

The Prof told Helga to set up a meeting with Quinton, James and Quanto their robotic assistant, she called them, and they arrived and joined them round the Prof extended desk. The Prof greeted them and said.

"Good morning, all, I have been able to continue contact with Freida my old-world secretary and admin manager and we have realised that we have a serious problem with our chip delivery to service the AI excessive humanoid power problem there on our old-world. She has been very helpful and practical, and I quote her last email in which she details how we can mutually deal with the delivery problem."

He paused and tapped on his keyboard and read out -

Ime locating suitable technicians to help me find and set up recall workshops in Germany and other counties and countries here on Earth. The long delivery times from Eunaton to just one workshop is inadequate and would become a constant problem with that just one chip delivery, and the power strikes will be constant and devastating and continue well into the future.

So hopefully in time we will have several workshops here on Earth installing the Neuron chips and helping to control the robot's AI excessive power consumption worldwide. Let's have your views about this and if you approve how will we pay for workshops and tools.

Regards Freida.

"We've thought about and talked about the delivery problem to the old-world before. Quinton said, and she's right, it's obvious that we've got to set up production there."

"I agree the prof said. And I've suggested that you, Freida and her future participants contact the management of the larger corporations and international businesses. Tel them that you are setting up a production facility to produce an advanced microchip that will control the excessive power consumption of their Humanoid robotic assistants and relieve them of the constant power strikes and emphasise your need to raise funds from all major organisations to get started."

"Yeah, James said with conviction. They should pay, all businesses and organisation that own and use humanoid assistants should be charged to receive the neuron chip and have it fitted both here and on the old-world."

"That's easier said than done. That means apart from setting up the production workshops we must organise sales and distribution administration." The Prof said.

"We've done that before. Quinton said. And Freida will be able to deal with admin and distribution in the old-world and we can deal with it here."

"Yes, the Prof said...opening his arms to emphasise. But first we must have the workshops and production facilities on the old world to make the microchips."

"Thats what Freida is trying to do. Said James. And we must now decide how we can help her to get started."

For a moment there was a pause as they all quietly contemplated the answer to the obvious question. Suddenly the Professor said.

"Helga, you and Christoph must join Freida in the old world to assist, advise and program my old workshop for the neuron microchip production. No questions, check the neuron algorithm update and prepare the appropriate production programme and book on the next bubble craft."

Christoph gulped, raised eyebrows and was about to say! as Helga loudly said.

"Right, everybody, let's get the gear and tools together we've got to get to the old world as soon as possible."

The Professor stood up and said.

"I'll email Freida, tell her your both be on your way and hopefully by the time you get there she may have the workshop ready to set up the plant for production."

"Well, she'll have a few months so hopefully we might have more than one workshop to set up." Christoph said, nodding his head and grinning. He suddenly looked up and said. "So, we all must use the original neuron algorithm parameters supplied by *RobotDigitel Mechanics to* make the chip. So, we must have an algorithm that can be defined as procedures and implemented as computer programs".

"It's a long process. Said Helga. It starts with the first Design and continues with step two Deposition continuing with Lithography, Etch, Ion Implantation, then the final process is the packaging including testing for Functionality and Quality before being packed and shipped to customers."

"Wow! said James. As he unplugged Helga's charging unit, coiled it and placed in her travel case, I can see now why you need a specially prepared algorithm to work with."

Christoff called.

"Come on the bubble craft is here, we've got to load the workshop gear."

"Yes, we've got to take the robotic operation computer software and one of the EUV printing machines." Helga said as she started to pack her smaller personal bag.

"Isn't Freida supposed to be getting and setting up the production and printing tools in the old-world workshop?"

"Yes James, but the EVU printers are very special and technical machines, and she would probably find it difficult to find one now in the old world."

"It's a good job we have a spare one here then."

The loading humanoids and crew looked so small as they busied themselves around the huge bubble craft in preparation for the next departure to the old world. A bubble minibus arrived discharging the prof, Helga, Christoff, James and Quinton. The Professor opened his arms hugging Helga saying.

"It's going to be a few months before you get there, look after yourself and use the journey time to work with Christoph and prepare yourselves to liaise with Freida and reestablish our old-world printing processes."

As he let go. He took out of his pocket his old-world bank debit card.

"Give this to Freida, he said, it will help her to find and purchase some of the tools needed in the old workshop. And use it pay for your hotel as well."

"Thanks Prof, said Helga with a big grin, we might be able to get a good night out with that as well." She said grinning purposefully.

"Good, yes, that would be my privilege." Said the Professor nodding his head with a big smile. "Get on that spacecraft and enjoy your visit".

She followed Christoph as they walked over to the bubble craft, they both turned and waved as they stepped on the boarding steps as the professor and the others waving back, saying, "Have a good trip, and James yelled. "Keep in touch whilst you're on the journey."

The doors closed as the boarding steps were removed and with its powerful sola powered thrusters the bubble craft slowly began to rise it looked so huge as it lifted and both Helga and Christof could be seen waving goodbye from one of the numerous seat windows.

The Prof, James and Quinton watched it for a while as it disappeared into the distant space. As they returned to their bubble car the Prof said.

"They've got a major job ahead of them, let's hope they don't have to many problems in getting the old-world production workshops set up."

"Well, Helga is not only a good programmer, but also a skilled technician and working with Christoff and Freida I don't think we have much to worry about."

Most of the passengers were sitting in the observation lounge taking in the changing scenery as the bubble craft silently rose through and above the cloudy atmosphere into the blue, white of space and as they looked down their new planet world 'Eunaton' came into view in all its glory showing the patchy changing colours as the planet continued to recede into the cloudy depth's

"Oh, it's so beautiful. "A lady passenger exclaimed" using her mobile to get a good shot before the colours began to blur."

"Yes, we're working hard to make it green." Said Helga as Christoff quietly said." And we're going to keep it green as well." Raising his phone and taking a photograph.

He emails the Prof.

HI all, Weve only been in flight about fifteen minutes, and we've seen our new world in colour for the first time, it's already becoming a beautiful green world, and we thank the old worlds humanoids for finding it and sending us here. Look at the photo, which really does not do it justice, but you'll get some idea of what our new planet looks like in space.... Christoff. He then sent a copy to his laptop and saved it to his document file with the caption '*New world photo re future blog and Eunaton report*'.

Later as the old world (Earth) came into view the brown patches of the southern areas were noticeable with just a few small green areas dotted around and Helga looked at Christoff as he said.

"It looks like the humanoids are controlling the basic causes of Earths climatic changes, having got rid of us together with the pollution, the diesel and petrol engines, air conditioners, and fridges et cetera. They now seem to have what they needed, the sun and daylight and a brighter cleaner working world ".

"Well, it will take at least a year or so if not more to get Earth back to its natural seasonal climatic environment". And they have yet to deal with enormous levels of Methane gases under the Seara dessert and the Earth's Oceans".

"They will. Helga commented. If you remember on our first flight to Eunaton the humanoid's would have seen the Russian scientist drilling through the ice on the Seira dessert, creating those huge gaseous flames from the methane as it was released under enormous pressure, and in the not too distant future with the gradual increase in climatic temperature change over time they predicted the ice would crack and the methane will be released and create huge devastating explosive fires."

"Well, I hope they do know what to do and how to prepare and prevent what could be a disastrous and devastating catastrophe. Said Christoff with conviction. I hope one day to retire back in my old-world German village, with clean air and pollution free."

Helga looked at him in surprise. "Really, don't you like your lovely new sun lit and sola powered domed home on our new planet."

"Yes, I do, and I like my work on Eunaton with you and the professor, but I am noting and recording the changes as we all mutually build our working, education and living environments in this changing new and different planet. And when I retire from my working life here, I intend to return to the old-world and write and create AI algorithms creating videos, software and reports about what we have all achieved here on Eunaton".

Helga stood up. "That sounds very presumptuous, she said, nodding her head and grinning. I'm going to order a coffee; would you like one?"

"Yes, with sugar, thanks". Christopher said nodding his head. As Helga walked away.

Tapping away on his laptop he wrote.

Working Title: Humanoid and Human AI educational sibling influence over the years.

Helga returned carrying two large plastic cups of coffee. She placed both on the small seat table and resumed her seat.

Christoff closed his laptop and said.

"With the rapid advancement and human use of robotic technology one cannot predict but only presume our technological future."

Helga sat quietly, clustered her hands on her chest, lowered her head and thought for a moment. Then picking up her coffee she said.

"And many will presume but very few will be right!"

"Maybe, but it's a long time into the future, by then us humans here, and in the old world together with the humanoids with the constant influence of AI we will all have changed beyond our apprehension, and by then both worlds will be living and working in a highly efficient and technically AI advanced environment".

"Well, a bit of that future technology depends now on us and our success in setting up our microchip printing in the old world, we should be there in a few days' time?"

"Yea' the captain should make an announcement soon".

Chapter 20.
Neuron Microchip production in the Old World.

On board the bubble craft the captain's voice came over the speakers.

"We are preparing to land on planet earth. All passengers please prepare your personal baggage and take a seat and securely fasten seatbelts. The weather is acceptable for landing, just a bit wet and windy. Your luggage will be unloaded and available in the arrival office."

"Uh! Same old world". Mumbled Christoff. Let's get our gear packed."

The observation lounge monitor screens were now showing closer views of planet earth revealing geographical images and shapes of the worlds numerous countries, rivers and oceans and as they got closer one was able to identify the large American, Russian and European areas as the bubble craft slowed and prepared to navigate to Spaytech's recommended landing region near the lunar South Pole. The captains voice came over.

"We are going to land near the Lunar South Pole and this specific landing site within this region will depend on the timing of the return launch window, ensuring our continued flexibility return flights throughout the year. And we are now about to fire our thrusters to slow down and enter Earth's atmosphere and our Heat Shield to protect our spacecraft from extreme heat during re-entry."

There appeared to be a lot of activity as they landed, and the captains voice came over and said.

"Please remain in your seats we need a few minutes to prepare to leave the spacecraft." Looking out the spacecraft window they saw a helicopter coming into land. As it landed, Freida and two young men stepped out. They saw the stationary Bubble craft, and Freida waved as she saw

the bubble craft passenger door slide open as they walked over to the arrival's office.

Helga and Christoff joined them in the arrival lounge. Freida hugged Helga saying.

"It's lovely to meet you both after all this time, you've had a long flight, we've ordered you both a coffee. How was the journey?"

"It was okay, we had to adjust sharing and living with two hundred other passengers in a small hotel environment for several months, but we were looked after quite well and the changing scenery of the stars, planets and those wonderful colourful views of our new planet as we left and seeing our old Earth from outer space as it came into view was very illuminating and we got some good photo's."

Christoff nodded, smiled and said.

"Yeah, I got some good shots and background notes on our new life on 'Eunaton.'"

"So, you had a good journey then." Commented Freida.

"Yes. Said Christoff, but he still a long journey, but with the latest solar power technology it has been reduced by at least a third of the original travel time."

And now we are going to work together again. She paused, gestured to her two companions' You may remember these two. This is Conrad and this is Anton, they both worked with us as technical assistants in our original workshop in Germany, and now there joining us to set workshops here in what you now call 'the Old World' ."

"Well nice to meet you again. Said Helga, you may also remember working with Christoff."

"Yes, we do, they shook hands all round." and Freida, commented.

"Well with us five we should have no problem in getting our microchip production set up again in our old workshop. So, let's get the next plane back to 'Frankfurt' and get that workshop into production."

"Weve got to find a hotel first. Said Christoff. And get our gear unpacked and I want to check my notes."

"Don't worry about that now, you can stay at our place tonight, and we can get you into a hotel tomorrow."

Chapter 21.
Old World microchip workshop set up.

It wasn't a long flight, they said goodbye at the airport to Anton and Conrad and took a cab to Freida's apartment. As Freida let them in, she said.

"I know it looks a bit small you can sleep in my big bed and Christoff can sleep on my bed settee."

"That sounds ok, with the money we're saving we can all go out for dinner tonight."

"No, I can cook for us, we don't need to go out."

"Yes, please take us to your favourite restaurant, I've got the professors old world debit card for to use on our hotel and restaurant expenses, So, come on, let us treat you."

"I know, let's go to the Lourds Hotel. We can get a good meal there and you could book your rooms there if you like it."

"That sounds okay, could I have a wash and change first?"

"Of course you can, I'll show you the bathroom and you can use my room to get changed."

Christoff said." And me, can I get changed in your room as well?"

"Yes, take your case in with Helga's but you will be sleeping here on the settee."

It was only a short walk to the Hotel, the restaurant seemed busy, but they were showed to a table and the nice young waitress with a big welcome smile asked.

"Would you like to order drinks first?"

Frieda looked at Helga who said.

"No, we'll wait until we have ordered."

The waitress nodded, smiled, turned and said.

"I'll get you the menu and wine list."

She returned with the menus and wine list saying.

" I'll be back in a few minutes."

Christoff ordered the fillet steak and the girls both ordered chicken breast with sauté potatoes. They each had the scampi cocktail starter. The waitress asked.

"Would you like to order a drink, now."

"Yes, said Helga. We'll have a bottle of Chardonnay to share."

"Thank you, would you like your wine now?"

"Yes. Said Helga. Make sure it's cool."

The waitress nodded her head and said.

"Yes of course."

Their prawn cocktails together with their wine was served and as the waitress upturned the wine glasses she said.

"Would you like me to pour your wine now."

"Yes please. Helga said." as Frieda and Christoff nodded.

As the waitress left Frieda picked up a glass and said.

"Here's to us three, and may we successfully recreate our production workshops and save both our planets form the disastrous consequences of the Humanoids artificial intelligent excessive power consumption."

Helga and Christoph raised their glasses, agreed and said.

"We will, and we can start tomorrow."

"Yes, said Frieda. Tomorrow we will meet Anton and Conrad and visit the old workshop and hopefully start to set it up ".

They each took a sip put down their glasses and started to enjoy their prawn cocktails.

Frieda said. "The Prof said he has sent some technical gear to help us to get started.?"

"Yes, we've got the robotic operation computer software and one of the EUV printing machines." Helga said.

"And we also have the necessary AI algorithm program files" Commented Christoff.

"Oh great, that's good. Anton will know how to set that up, and we all know how to use the software. So, we'll soon have the old workshop back in production." Freida said, showing her enthusiasm.

Their dinner was served and Christoff said.

"My steak looks good. Picking up his knife and fork cutting a small piece.

Yea, it's done just the way I like it."

Frieda started to serve the sauté potatoes and said.

"Well, they have a good chef, and we come here quite often."

"It smells and looks good, lets enjoy it."

Helga said cutting a slice of her roast chicken.

"We could probably stay here." Commented Christoff.

"Well, we can check the rooms and cost before we leave and come back and book tomorrow if okay."

"It is quite expensive to stay here. But I know the Manager I could ask him if it's possible to get a long stay discount."

"Well, I think we're going be here for some time, but how long is difficult to predict". Said Helga.

Christof intervened and said.

"We are hoping to find and set up at least two or three workshops, so I reckon will be here at least a couple of months."

"Well, said Helga. The food is good, let's enjoy it then we 'll have a coffee in the lounge and check out the room costs before we leave."

So, they each finished their dinner with a fruit cocktail and left to have a coffee in the lounge area.

There were a few hotel guests sitting around and they found a suitable table. Sitting down Frieda said.

"I'll go over to reception and order our coffee and ask to see the manager."

As she walked over to the reception counter she was obviously well known as the receptionist was pleased to see her could be heard asking her how she was.

Their coffee was served and over at reception Freida was talking to the hotel manager, and he was seen to be smiling and nodding his head in agreement to whatever Freida was saying.

Frieda returned with a big grin on her face, opened her arms and said.

"It was very understanding of the important work we are doing, and he said that if your stay here is longer than three weeks then he will discount your food bill by 20% and your two rooms discounted by 10%."

"That's good. Said Helga. We're going to be here longer than three weeks so let's look at the rooms and we can book before we leave."

"Yeah okay, drink up, let's look now." Said Christof standing up and gulping his coffee.

They booked two single rooms with breakfast and evening dinner.

Back in Frieda's apartment Helga gave Freida a big hug…saying.

" Thanks, you're so helpful, you've got us a good deal from the hotel Manager, thanks." Showing her satisfaction with a final squeeze.

Freida pulled out the sofa bed and said.

"Christoff, I'll get you a pillow and blanket, it's quite a comfortable bed."

"Yeah, it's big enough for two." Said Helga.

I will just email the professor then we're off to bed, the bathroom is first door on the right in the hall, you go in first."

"Okay, I'll have a quick shower and see you both in the morning. Thanks Frieda, good night."

Frieda picked up her laptop and said as she walked to her room. "Hope you have a good sleep. We're going to be busy tomorrow."

Hi Prof. She typed

We have some good news. I met Helga and Christoff at reception in the terminal lounge and introduced the too Anton and Conrad who remember both worked for you as production technicians. We also have the other two I told you about, Gary and Les, making four of your ex-technicians here ready to help us. We're meeting them tomorrow at your old workshop and we're going to start setting up the workshop. We've got an electrician to check and monitor the existing power supply. We may be able to install the EVU printer tomorrow which will be a good start as the clean room is still as we left it with the working desktops and ready for replacing the robotic machines, computers, and printer installations. I'll keep you informed.

Regards Frieda.

The Professor replied almost instantly.

Hi Frieda,

Glad to see you are getting so well organised. The technicians together with Helga and Christoph will know where to order the robotic equipment and the suppliers will have a installation adviser to help with the initial robotic setup. And you can use my card to pay for the equipment hopefully they will have all that you need in stock, otherwise there will be a possible few days' delay. You also need to contact our old-world suppliers and order the integrated circuit RFID device encased in silicate glass that may take a while as well. They may need to talk to me about the RFID specification if they do you can give them my contact address...Thanks, you're getting a good team together...Prof.

She sent a copy to Helga's and Christoph's laptops and typed.

Just got a reply from the professor, will discuss this in the morning... Frieda.

After a hurried breakfast they discussed the Professors email instructions and suggestions, and Frieda called Anton and Conrad.

"We're just about to leave we'll meet you at the workshop, bring your laptops. Frieda".

Helga and Christoff both checked their computer files and unpacked the all-important EUV printer. Frieda was pleased to find the old workshop account files on her computer and said with satisfaction.

"Got it. I've found the suppliers for the silicate glass RFID circuits let's hope they have them in stock".

"Good". Helga said as they left for the workshop.

Anton and Conrad were already there waiting for them after the Hi's and Good mornings. Frieda unlocked the door, and they all trooped in.

As Frieda had said. The workshop had been left just as the professor and his team had evacuated it. Petitioning, clean room, workbenches office desks all clean and ready for use.

Helga walked over and said.

"This was my desk, and I can plug in now and start to use it." Placing her computer on the desk.

Christoph did the same. Walked over to his original workspace placed his laptop on his desk and bent down and looked underneath to check the power supply. He plugged in just has Frieda pulled down the mains power switch above the door and his power supply point red light came on.

Both Anton and Conrad were both curious, they walked and looked around and Conrad said.

"Looks like when we get the tools and printer setup we could be in business in no time."

"Yes. Said Frieda. Do you know how to install the printer."

"Yes, once it's plugged in, I can download the instruction manual."

"Right, let's do it now."

Christoph grinned and said. "Yes, let's get this setup and placed the printer on the original workbench. Conrad immediately threaded the power plug through the cable hole and pulled a chair over sat down and said.

"Keep your fingers crossed, I hope it's okay."

Helga busy on her computer suddenly yelled out.

"Fantastic, they've got the RFID circuits in stock, and they have accepted the professors debit card. And they will deliver tomorrow before twelve."

Christoph looked over and said.

"That's good, things are beginning to come together."

"Yes, I've now got to locate the robotics suppliers." Helga said.

"Make sure they send a technician to help us when they deliver." Christoff said emphatically. And added...

"The Professor said they will send an adviser to help us with the initial setup". "Yes, they will". Helga said continuing tapping away on her laptop.

Anton asked," What about the silicon wafer processes where do we get the silicon wafer board. Did we have an account for it".

"Yes, we did have an account and will probably be able to find it, but first I want to get the robotic equipment ordered."

Conrad loudly and finally clicked his keyboard and said.

"That's it, the printers okay and ready for the Microsoft printing software."

"That's great, we're getting organised and when the robotic tools arrive it won't take long to get set up for production." Frieda said nodding her head, smiling and showing her satisfaction.

"Well, we've got the RFID software and hopefully we'll have the robotic installation and operative software in the next day or so we could be in production in a couple of days." Added Helga.

"Yes. Christoff said. Tapping away on his laptop. We don't have any robotic software files, so I expect all comes with robotic machinery."

"Well yes, it does. The delivery technicians will have the necessary auxiliary computers together with all the operational software, so you don't need to worry about that, just hope that we find and get access to the manufacturers original account with us."

"Right Helga, keep looking, if we can get the robotics delivered and set up then all we need is the silicon wafer board and we're ready to go."

Helga suddenly called Frieda.

"You used to deal with business accounts did you have a bookkeeping file? "

"Yeah, I kept the accounts in a daybook accounting database."

"Would you still have access to that file."

"No, but it could be still available on the professor's computer."

"Right, emailing now ask him."

It didn't take long they got a reply within a few minutes.

Hi Frieda,

You should have asked me earlier. The manufacturing and supply company is 'Robotics Interactive Inc'. I have emailed them and reestablished our account and ordered the necessary robotic equipment to get you started. You should hear from them soon with a delivery date. Keep up the good work and keep me informed of your progress... Prof.

The same day Frieda received an email from Robotics Interactive Inc.

Hi Mdm Frieda,

We are pleased to have accepted a repeat order for the robotic machinery and installation equipment. Delivery and assisted installation will be tomorrow before noon...please reply and confirm acceptance.

Regards,

Bernhard

Delivery Manager.

Frieda replied.

Hi Bernhard,

Thank you for your email we look forward to your delivery tomorrow please insure that we have some initial installation assistance.

Regards,

Frieda.

Hi Frieda,

Yes Frieda, we allow the driver technician maximum one hour to assist you in installation of the robotic equipment.

Regards, Bernhard.

Chapter 22.
Old World Neuron chip production.

The robotics arrived, and a very pleasant young man (Max) asked.

"Can I have someone to help me to unload"

Christoff said. "Yeah okay, let's get it in."

And it wasn't long before the machines and operational computers were in place, and it was quite exciting as they were plugged in and both Frieda and Helga couldn't wait to get Max to start and initialise the computers and prepare for production programming.

Max was an experienced robotic installation technician and was able to show and talk them through the computer programming and robotic installation which took some time, and he left them with the installation manuals and his email and website for when and as needed.

Christoff and Helga now sitting in their original seats both felt quite confident that they will soon be capable of printing their microchip products here in the old world again. Christoph said.

"That's why the Professor sent us, he knew that once we were set up our experience would take over and we'd be confident to deal with the production of our microchips here in the old world."

"Yes, it's strange I'm beginning to feel as if I have never left this, and I thought I am ready to get on with my production programming."

"Yeah, I feel the same first we need to order the silicon sheets and the delivery packaging. Can you do that Helga or get Frieda to do it."

Frieda heard that, looked up and said.

"Don't worry, I've already done that, we expect delivery some time tomorrow. And I'm just about to email the prof and tell him we now have the robotics set up."

"He'll be pleased to hear that. Said Helga, tell him we're ready to start the process of manufacturing the digital microchip layers and we're just waiting for the silicon wafer board and Conrad may have found a workshop in Berlin."

Frieda tapped away and the email was sent.

The Prof replied.

Hi Frieda, it seems like your efforts are getting the old workshop back together quite efficiently with the robotic equipment set up and the printers synchronised then you're ready to go. But it is now important that you, Helga and Christoph when you receive delivery of your silicon wafer boards you take note to ensure that the printers are prepared for the long and critical ultraviolet layered processes that you are about to experience. I enclose a copy of the EUV printing process which I want you three to read again and understand how critical the printing process is and please let me know when you're ready to print...Regards Prof.

The process of manufacturing a digital microchip involves hundreds of steps and can take up to four months from design to mass production. The process starts with building up layers of interconnected patterns and silicon wafer. And different types of lithography systems are used for different layers. Critical layers with the smallest features are printed using EUV (extreme ultraviolet) while the less critical layers with larger features are printed using EUV (deep ultraviolet) machines.

Frieda replied.

Thanks Prof. I remember how we were all concerned how long it used to take to print out our microchips but, as then we will use the time to prepare the packaging as Helga concentrates on building up layers of interconnected patterns and silicon wafer and hopefully we will eventually produce and continue to produce enough of the neuron microchips to cope with the robotic installations here in Frankfurt and eventually in the proposed workshop to be set up by Conrad in Berlin .

That's good news, replied the Prof. *keep me informed if you get the Berlin workshop, I will need to provide the funds to get it set up.*

Helda and Christoph both busy on their computers checking and preparing the notes and appropriate programs in preparation for the long and critical printing process. Christoph stopped and said.

"I think we got a problem".

"Why, what you found."

"It's something to do with human safety precautions."

Helda picked up the installation manual, thumbing through she said.

"There's nothing here, no reference to human safety at all."

"Let's ask Max." Christoph said looking for his email address.

Hi Max,

Big problem can't complete the printer setup something to do with human safety there is no reference to human safety in the software or in the printer manuals.

Please advise ASAP

regards. Christoph.

It wasn't long before Max replied.

Your Looking in the wrong place your robotics installation automatically deals with the EUV extreme and deep ultraviolet applications, and you need to link into the robotic set up program and locate the EUV human safety link and ensure that it is operation. Safety operation is very important so get back to me to let me know that the safety link is operational... Max.

Christopher did not feel very confident as he investigated the robotic machinery set up program which appeared to be very technical, and he could not find the human safety link that Tim had referred to.

Helga tried and worked on her computer for some time, but she also found it difficult and, in the end, gave up and said.

"Let's get back to Max, he'll know what to do."

She emailed.

Hi Max,

We have both found the robotic installation program very technical and have not been able to find the safety link you referred to can you get back and tell us what we need to look for…. Helga.

Max replied instantly.

Hi,

I agree, it is a bit technical the safety link is within the algorithm, and I should have checked the safety link was activated when we set up the installation program. Sorry about that. Anyway, we can sort this out together, have you got TeamVieiw on your computer. If you have set it up and we can get online together, talk and exchange ID number and passwords. Max.

"That's good. Said Christoph. Here we are back in the old world and I'm using teamview. Tim is telling me not to use my mouse as he wants to control my computer with his mouse."

"Well, with teamview one is allowed to remotely control a distant computer, he's going to get into the robotic program and show us how to find that safety link." Said Helga as Max came on and said.

"Right, see that cross symbol to the top left, as he moved the curser. That's the safety link, click on it now."

Christoff clicked and up came 'EUV human safety link is activated.

"There you are. Said Max. Your now able to operate your printers."

"Thanks Max, now we can use TeamView we feel confident that we have your technical support as we got through the long and arduous process of finally setting up the robotics and printers for our microchip production. We would like to meet you socially and treat you to a meal one evening. and if okay we could meet at the Lourds Hotel say Saturday evening at a time to suite you.

"Yeah, I would like to know how you got on with the printing, 7:30 at Lourd's would be fine, thanks Chris See you then. Got to go, talk soon."

"Good, said Frieda, we can all go, we are a team now that will be six of us with Tim, that's going to cost a few euros. Good job Helga's got the Professor's debit card, she said we could use it for the hotel and all other expenses."

Anton said." I've got 50 euro's that will pay for mine and a bottle of wine."

"No keep that for another time. Helga said. The Professor said we could use it for a night out. Right now, we've got to get on with the printing set up, I've already linked into the printing software?"

The silicon board arrived later that day and a few hours later the printers were finally ready to productive printing.

Frieda emailed the Prof.

Hi Pro,

Were done, the robotics and printers finally co-ordinated and ready for microchip production, we have the silicon wafers, and we are now preparing to start the printing process. We've got a good team here together now with Anton and Conrad who will learn the productive processes and eventually be ready to control and set up the workshop in Berlin.

As usual the Professor was quick to reply.

Hi Frieda... Thanks for keeping me updated, so your about to start the printing of the neuron microchip in our old world, well done, it will take a couple of months to process the chips, but that will give you the chance and the time for you and Anton to hopefully get that workshop set up in Berlin. You have adequate funds with my debit card to cover the set-up expenses as needed. Please ask Helga to email me, we miss them both and we would like to know how they are getting on.

Chapter 23.
Old world chip production.

As they took their seats around a big circular table in the hotel restaurant the waiter came over and said. "Good evening, Mme Frieda, nice to see you again can I leave you with the menus."

"Yes thanks, is there anything special tonight."

"Yes, we have a special English dish. Scottish smoked salmon with a king prawn and crab sauce with sauté potatoes and fresh English garden peas and served with a mushroom pate starter."

They looked at each other, grinned and Freida said, "That sounds good, shall we have that."

They agreed and Helda said. "That will be nice with a bottle white Sauvignon. "

"That's a good choice, said the waiter, I'll make sure it's cool."

Their Pate starter was served by the young waitress who remembered them, saying. "Nice to see again, I see you've ordered the fish, you'll enjoy that." As the waiter turned up and poured the wine.

They sat and chatted amongst themselves enjoying their meal as Frieda raised her glass and said.

""Well, here's to us, we've been very busy over the last few weeks but tomorrow we shall have our printing machines ready to start the long printing process so all we need to do now is to relax and prepare the wafer board to start printing."

"Yes, thanks to you two, commented Anton looking at Helda and Christoff, without you two we could never have achieved the technical set up without your help and experience."

"That's okay, your just recapping on your past experience and you'll soon be setting up the production unit in Berlin with Conrad."

"Yeah, we're looking forward to that, and you're not too far away to help and advice if needed."

Max stood up clinked his glass and said.

"Here's to you all, you're doing a fantastic job here in producing a microchip that will control the excessive AI power consumption within the Robotic Humanoids algorithm. and eliminating the continual and devastating power strikes we are all continually experiencing as our humanoid assistants use the quantum power of Artificial Intelligence."

He paused for a moment, raised is glass and continued.

"And we can thank you for that and I thank you for inviting me. That's one of the best meals I've had and it's good to hear that your set up and ready for microchip production. And please consider me as part of the team and call on me if you have any problems with your robotics and printers. So, here's to us and our microchip productive future... Cheers." They raised their glasses and unanimously said.

"To us." And looked at each other and took a good sip from their glasses.

"You're right. Said Frieda. We are going to be jointly instrumental in successfully controlling the excessive power consumption of working humanoids, let's have another drink to that."

Having enjoyed a good evening together they left the hotel in a happy mood ready for an early night and knowing that tomorrow all the past trials and tribulations would have come to a head as Helga said ...

"Tomorrow we will start printing and making the neuron chip here in this old world of ours." Showing her feelings gesticulating with open arms with a big smile on her face.

"Yeah, Frieda said with resignation in her voice. At last, I'll email the Professor."

"What time is it now on our new world 'Eunaton?" asked Helga.

"It's about midday there now". Exclaimed Christoph.

"That's okay, I'll email him as soon as we get in."

The Professor's watch buzzed. *You've got mail.* He clicked on his keyboard and quickly read Frieda's email

Hi Professor,

We've just enjoyed a good dinner at the hotel with Max as our guest as he has been so helpful in the technical application of our robotics. And he asked us to accept him as part of our team here and he is ready to work with Anton and Conrad when they have access to the workshop in Berlin.

We are ready to start printing here but we've still got to select and prepare the silicon wafer boards but we anticipate starting production tomorrow. Helga and Christoph will work with us for a couple of days and then they will be ready to take the long journey back to Eunaton. We will miss them they've been very helpful in supervising the setup of our workshop. They will contact you when their ready to come back. Regards Frieda.

He paused for a moment and decided to email Tim.

Hi Tim...I'm pleased to say they have set up and ready to start chip production back in the old-world workshop and have another workshop about to be set up in Berlin. As you know it's a very long process involving hundreds of steps and it's going to take at least four months before the printers are ready to produce any chips. In the meantime, that give us a chance to send urgent chip orders to both workshops whilst waiting for the long EUV printing process to take its course and hopefully a chance to get your workshop set up in the old world as well. Keep in touch, regards Prof.

Tim replied.

Hi Prof,

Thanks for the info, Ime pleased to say that Carl is now in the process of setting our first small factory unit to accept and install our neuron chip in the old worlds recalled robotic humanoids so as you say you need to send your microchips to get our workshops started whilst they wait for their printers to begin the chip production. In the meantime, I'll find out the next delivery date for the old world. Regards Tim.

The Prof briefly replied.

Thanks Tim, let's have the date when you get it, I'm pleased you got your factory set up in the old- world we can now jointly control the humanoid power problem... Great, Prof.

The next day the professor got an email from Hilda.

We're leaving here later today, and Christoph said that now with the latest solar assisted bubble craft we'll be home in less than a year... Hilda.

A few days later Christoph emailed the Professor and said.

This new bubble craft is fantastic, apart from luxury living quarters its speed with its hybrid solar and oxygenated gas thrusters is astronomical and the captain said that the ETA for Eunaton should be less than nine months. Look forward to seeing you all then. Regards Christoph.

Time went by and James got an email from Hilda.

Hi, it won't be long now before we see each other again, we expect to arrive about midday your time tomorrow, how have you been, I've missed you and I'm dying to see you...Hilda.

The Prof was impressed and said.

"Are you sure he said tomorrow, that's less than nine months, its only eight months and three weeks."

"Well, they're on the latest hybrid solar bubble craft which is apparently very fast."

"Yeah, it must be, if you remember the journey took us more than two years." He said nodding his head in contemplation.

"Yes, I do, answered James. It seemed like a lifetime."

"Ime glad to have them back, the office hasn't been the same without them."

Hilda and Christoph stepped out the bubble craft, Hilda waved as James, Quinton and the Professor waved to them from the steps of the reception lounge. They walked over and joined them and after hugs all round they took off in the bubble car back to the Professor's office.

"I suppose your pleased with the two new productive workshops we now have in the old world."

"Yes Hilda, it was a necessity, and you've all done so well to get out chip production back into the old - world."

"Frieda was very conscientious and together with the other two were able to set up the workshop up from scratch, and now their printing away as we sit here."

"Yes, Frieda has been very helpful and efficient, she not only found two technicians for the old workshop, but she also found Anton and Conrad who are now setting up a Berlin workshop."

"She enjoys her work. Christoph said. And she's very concerned about the AI power problem with robotic humanoids. And by now she will be preparing and organising the actual installation of the neuron chip in the humanoid robots all now still lined up like soldiers in the workshop."

"We must somehow show our appreciation". The Prof said.

"I know, I've got an idea". Quinton said.

"Yeah, what." The Prof asked.

"She's worked with us from the beginning in the old-world and wants to stay involved and so continues to uphold our team spirit and expects to be part of our technical and social planning here on our new planet."

"What do you suggest then." The Prof asked as he turned parking the bubble car on the green in front of his office.

"Well as you know, Quinton said. Apart from the AI power problem we've got to think about the implications of AI social effects within the human social communities so why not invite Frieda over here join us in an AI future project."

"I'm glad you said that the Prof said. I've already made some notes about the future of AI and inviting Frieda over here to take part in that project is a good idea."

Chapter 24.
The future of Artificial Intelligence.

A few months later Freida arrived and was welcomed back into the Professors team. Back in the Profs office with Hilda and Christoph back and Frieda now joining them James found an extra chair and they all sat round the professors extended desk.

The Prof said. "It's good now we are altogether again and we welcome Frieda and thank her for her superb technical and efficient application of setting up our microchip production workshops back in the old world."

"Thank you for that. Said Frida. Nodding...and smiling".

"Now we've got AI under our control. Continued the Prof, we've got to think about the potential of AI's future and its ability to create facts, figures and answers to all the problems within the human living and working environment.

"What! Asked James. That could be another project."

"As I've just said. Everything and anything" Said the prof, shrugging his shoulders, just ask 'Quanto.'"

"Yeah okay." Said James's walking over to the window.

"Quanto wake up"

"*Yes, my Master.*"

"Quanto, will AI influence our future applications and impact our social and working lives."

"*Yes certainly. Artificial intelligence (AI) is rapidly shaping and changing your international worlds, and its future applications are diverse and impactful. Here are the key areas where AI will play a significant role:*

__Business Automation:__ Approximately 55% of organizations have already adopted AI to varying degrees. As a result, we can expect increased automation across various business processes. Chatbots and digital assistant's handle simple customer *reactions, while AI analyses vast amounts of data to provide instant insights for decision making.*

Healthcare: *AI can revolutionize healthcare by combining human intuition with precision. Imagine doctors using AI to assist in diagnosis, treatment planning, and personalized medicine.*

Finance and Investments: *AI algorithms can analyse financial data, predict market trends, and optimize investment portfolios. This technology enhances decision-making and risk management.*

Linguistics: *AI-powered language models improve natural language understanding, translation, and sentiment analysis.*

Anti-Collision Technology: *AI can enhance safety in vehicles by providing collision avoidance systems. These systems use sensors and AI algorithms to prevent accidents.*

Remember, AI's impact extends across various domains, including healthcare, education, manufacturing, virtual assistance, and entertainment.

While some goals, like replicating human activity human creativity and modelling consciousness, remain distant. AI continues to evolve and shape our future.

"Well, there you are, that's what we can expect to experience in the not-too-distant future." The Prof said with that knowing look on his face.

He paused for a moment and then said.

"It's been long time since we started controlling the robots and most of them in the old-world and on Eunaton here are now fitted with the neuron chip. And the excessive power use is now under control and is now virtually eliminating the constant power strikes."

"Yes" said Quinton, but we must keep checking the humanoids on a regular basis to make sure that the neuron chip remains compatible with humanoid algorithms."

"Yes, said James. That will have to be done by the owners of the humanoid robots."

"Yeah, but it could be possible to program the humanoids to self-check on a regular basis".

"Well, if we can do that. Said James, then that's the answer to the neuron production compatibility problem."

"Yeah okay, I'll check the parameters and see if we could create a humanoid self-checking algorithm." Said Hilda.

"That's another project for you Hilda. The humanoids can be programmed for self-checking. Said the Professor. In the meantime, I've got to think about the AI future and send a copy of Quanto's predictions to Tim".

The Prof emailed Tim at *RobotDigitel Mechanics.*

Hi Tim,

Have you had a chance to read a copy of Quanto's AI future predictions...Prof.

Tim answered immediately.

Yes Prof, I'm a bit concerned how our manufacturers, the old-world governments and social organisation are going to cope with the imminent predicted changes AI is going to make within our business and social environment."

Prof replied. *That's what I want to talk about I suggest we have a meeting to discuss how we are going to prepare for the AI future.*

Yeah, I agree, I'll come to your office how about later today, say about three -o-clock...Regards Tim.

The Professor opened the meeting with a profound statement.

"The future of AI is going to create a lot of changes in the robotic industries and the microchip manufacturing industry, and you make the robots, and we make the microchips that go in them. So, we will both be affected by the AI's future, so we need to discuss and hopefully anticipate the future productive changes needed in our businesses."

"Well, if what your Quanto predicted then there will be an enormous amount of changes in the digital, computer and AI applications and we need to act now on a mutual plan to incorporate those changes."

"Yeah, there's more to the future of AI as one realises, said the Prof, and we as professional computer technicians are going to be needed, and we'll need to work together as a joint organization planning, designing and producing new powerful future AI microchips. And we'll need a DUV (deep ultraviolet printing machine) and your robotic computer interfaces will all need new algorithm instructions and be reprogrammed."

"Yes, I expected that, but I also think that driverless cars, lorries, busses and even trains will change, they will be auto built with an AI robotic driver and there will not be any need for human drivers at all within the transport industry. And the present human use of personal transport will not be needed, and we will have access to standby robotic vehicles at will and paid for by a road and transport tax with a mobile phone licence with a personal password to activate it for those that will want or need transport at any time.

The professor slowly nodded his head as Tim continued.

"That's where our business acumen comes in, we'll need your AI chips to produce our robotic drivers controlling their sensors and camera's."

"Yeah, and that's only one obvious change we must consider, said Prof, think about the Financial, Medical, and Educational and other digital, computer and robotic changes that will need to me made."

"Yes, we need to get our staff teams together, Tim said and let them know we are now working mutually to plan for the AI future digital and robotic changes, and they will need to liaise with each other with a daily report as they mutually exchange information and write and prepare the changes that will be needed with the algorithm parameters."

"Yeah, they've worked together before with the humanoid power problem, the prof said. So, there will be no problem in us all working together."

"Just think what could happen. Said Tim. What it means to humanity as we work together, the two of us with our teams we will all be creating the human and the humanoid artificial intelligent future for all humanity. So, let's get a meeting set up today whilst I'm here, I'll get my manager and his technical assistance over here, they could be here within the hour."

"Right the first thing we must do is to prepare a list of what we want to achieve, said the Prof, before they get here".

"Okay, but first we need is to print out copies of Quanto's AI futures list as everyone will need to refer to it as we discuss and plan how we are going to prepare for AI future applications."

It wasn't long before Mark Tim's production manager and Len his technical assistant arrived, they were quickly introduced, and Frieda handed out the AI future list as they all sat round the Prof's extended desk.

So, there they all were. The Professor, Quinton, James, Hilda, Christoff, Frieda, Tim, Mark and Len. Not one of them realised that they were about to make AI controlling decisions that were to make AI technical history.

"Okay. The Prof said, you've all got a copy of the proposed AI Social, Medical and Economic future applications, read it and understand that our future social, working and business lives will radically change as AI's future applications take effect. So, we are now here to discuss, plan and make notes in preparation for the algorithm parameters needed for AI future applications."

"Yes. Said Tim. Were need the microchips as soon as possible, so we've must get some of the parameters done now, today."

"Yeah, your first job Tim, is to produce the robotic automatic system for self-driving cars, so we'll get the microchips to you as soon as we know how to make them."

"Okay. Tim said. Let's get our heads down and get on with it, it's going to take some time especially your DUV micro printing process."

The meeting went on for several hours and at times became quite argumentative, both the Prof and Tim knowing their microchip and robotic technical limitations were able to mutually control the parameter notes and suggestions. And at the end of a long but very positive meeting they produced AI technical parameters to accommodate the preparation of the algorithms needed to facilitate the transport, medical, social and financial future AI applications.

As they were leaving the meeting the Prof said.

"As we have mutually agreed to work together It's important that we keep in touch with each other daily and Tim and I will produce a daily report as we work and prepare the algorithms between ourselves".

Frieda having been the Professors secretary in the old-world for many years was pleased to be part of the Profs team again and naturally resumed her assistive admin duties within the team's working environment. The Prof noticed and said.

"It's like it used to be, Frieda. Knowing how we used to work together you have again proved to be a much-needed asset within the team."

"Thanks Prof, it's good to be involved you have a very important robotic programming project involving a lot of intensive digital computing and I want to help as much as possible."

"Well, you are. As I have just said, you've already proved that you understand what we must achieve as quickly as possible. So, we all appreciate your help, and I am so glad you joined us."

Back in Tim's office they could be seen with their heads down tapping away on their computers and Tim was cooperating with the Professor both live on their computers with 'Teamview'. As time went on it was good to see the activity of both teams working in mutual corporation and over the next two days, they began to get the necessary algorithm parameters together and the microchip and robotic interfaces started to be prepared for production. After the usual edits and changes the Professor showing his relief continued typing away vigorously and sent an email.

To All,

Good and thank you, we've all done so well, we can now prepare the algorithms in preparation for the AI future social business software and the applications for reprogramming our robotic machinery and our humanoid robotic assistants.

Thank you all for your personal efforts and my regards to you all for what has been a complicated, and technically intensive project.

And we've now done it, thanks.

Professor Hindenburg.

Quinton said as he read the email.

"From that it appears that we can now conclude that we have done what was necessary and have achieved what we expected and anticipated, and that we have now protected our human social and living environment so we can now use the AI in all our social, education and financial and business applications with assurances and confidence".

"Well, we have. Said James. Looking at the Professor. We can thank the Professor and Tim for that."

"Yes, but as I said. Nodding his head and smiling with gratitude. All of you made and contributed completion of the algorithms for the AI future applications."

"Yes Pro, said Hilda. But it was you and Tim, your initial planning and enthusiasm that encouraged us to get on with the production of those parameters and algorithms."

"Maybe, said Tim. But it was all your collective team spirit that got the job done so successfully."

"Never mind that. Exclaimed Quinton. We know we all did a good job but now we must prepare and plan for that long process of printing the new microchips."

"Yeah, but first we gotta load our printer with the extra powerful EUV printer driver, without that you can't start anything". Said James.

"Yes, we have that 'extreme ultraviolet' driver file link so that can soon be loaded."

The professor said, tapping away on his computer.

"Let's have it, Prof. I can load it." Hilda said opening her laptop.

The Professor said, as he tapped away.

"Yeah, I've got it, Hilda you'll have in a few seconds."

The EUV printer driver was successfully loaded, and the Prof said.

"Okay, we all know our duties, so let's get back to work as Tim and I set out mutually working programs for the printing and Tims robotic production "I know how well you all know your old- world positions ,so let's get on with it..

As they left the meeting Frieda asked the Professor.

"Can I help with setting up the microchip planning process as I used too."

"Of course, Frieda, you will be a great help we have a lot of digital micro design and planning to do, and Hilda will love to have you work with her".

Mark and Len getting back to Tim's workshop decided to review their robotic production interfaces and prepare for the new AI algorithms and what will eventually be new and different robotic future production systems.

Tim got back a bit later and was pleased to see them working on the robotic productive computers and said.

"I see you've started already, what are you working on?"

"We're looking at the new algorithmic interfaces for the new robotic auto self-drive vehicles. The first impression is they appear to be on a higher digital level and a bit complicated."

"Off course, what do you expect, it's our new AI self-drive algorithm you've got to study it for a while first, then follow the instructions and learn how to apply it to the new productive interfaces and load the files into the robotic production computers.

So, get your heads down and work out the productive processes for our new automatic self-drive on demand vehicle hire robotic driver".

"If it's just going to be used for vehicle hiring how that going to work for personal transport"? asked Len.

"We dealt with that at the meeting, and I will remind you".

"When you need a car, van, lorry bus, train it will be supplied by the manufacturer and will be paid for by a road, rail and transport tax with a mobile phone transport licence app, each will have a personal password to activate it and charge by the mile or kilometre for those that will want or need to hire any form of transport for any distance at any time".

"Yeah, so anyone with a mobile phone can hire a car, what about the underage kids and the elderly"?

"Well Len, there will have to be some form of age ID and an automatic check on the financial ability of the hirer."

"So really. Said Mark. We will not be able to buy a car for personal use."

"No and you won't need too, your future transport and travel use will be available as needed and hassle free and much cheaper as there will no personal fuel, insurance or maintenance which you would have to pay if you owned a car."

"I think that will alleviate most of the major and accident problems we had on the old-world." Said Mark.

"It certainly will. Said Len. And our new Auto self- drive robots we are about to produce will be in total control of the vehicle, accident free and saving a lot of lives".

"It will be more than a major improvement. Said Tim. It will create a new and different national and international transport environment throughout the social and business communities".

"Yeah, Mark said. National governments and local councils will all need to change the usual by-laws, licences and transport litigation and work within the AI applications. And as self-driving technology progresses, robust regulatory frameworks will be essential to ensure safety and ethical operation. Governments and organizations are working on creating standards and guidelines to manage these vehicles so in the future we will eventually have a more efficient friendly transportation environment to live and work with."

"Right let's get on with it, the quicker we get these computers set up the quicker we'll be able to start producing what is going to be the first AI vehicle self-drive robot."

Tim said as he sat down and clicked on his keyboard and emailed the Professor.

Hi Prof,

Weve done a good job with the Algorithms, especially for our new auto self-drive vehicle units, my manager and Len originally thought the new AI applications were more technically advanced in comparison in what they've been used to, but after further examination they both got quite excited and are now preparing to program our robotic production computers, so we need your AI microchips as soon as possible, were going to produce a robotic auto self-drive unit that will change the world of automotive manufacturing and create a personal, social and business environment throughout the words transport organisations.

Regards Tim

The Prof answered.

Tim, that's some statement, I feel as excited as you and your team appear to be, were doing the same, were setting up the DUV printers and preparing the silicon wafers and hopefully we can start printing in a couple of days, we understand the urgency to get started and we will do our best to get the chips to you as soon as we can. In the meantime, I've attached a copy of an announcement that Quinton recorded last night from the old-world, a government minister in London, England on AM STAT news had said.

I'd like to have your views on what appears to be an international thank you. ¶

Regards Prof.

Copy from Quinton:

I have recorded what I heard last night on 'AM Stat News'.

We must thank Professor Hindenburg and RoboDigitel Mechanics Inc and their technical teams way back a few multi-million light years away on their new planet Eunaton. They have created and produced the AI algorithms for the control and maintenance of the software and robotic programming for the imminent future AI applications that is to affect us all in our social, educational and financial lives. And in addition, they have saved our world and their new world the disastrous and continuous power strikes so recently created by the excessive power use of Artificial Intelligence by the

Robotic Humanoids. Their new neuron microchip with a technically advanced algorithm is a creative necessity to control the excessive power consumption of our working Robotic Humanoids. And we all gratefully thank them for their relentless continued efforts for their technical achievements for our future control of Artificial Intelligence.

The Professor heard back from Tim and to quote, he said.

"It's obvious to me Pro, that our work has been approved and recognised within the legitimate and technically advanced fraternity within the quantum physical world and it's good to know that a senior English Government Minister has been prepared to make such a positive and appreciative statement about our work in the artificial intelligent control and use of our robotic humanoid assistants.

It is without doubt that we have both achieved what his statement said, we have saved our worlds from what could have been imminent and excessive power control of artificial intelligence by our robotic humanoids. And I now look forward to mutually working with you again as we analyse and determine the future of Artificial Intelligence".

The prof agreed and answered.

"Thanks Tim, yes, it's more than an international thank you, it is a universal acknowledgement that artificial intelligence is in its early stages of the unique use of quantum physics and beginning to work beyond the boundaries of human intelligence with new and unique aspirations creating the AI future technology.

And I too look forward to our work together as we seek to control the future imminent social, working, corporate and business AI applications."

Regards Prof.

At a later meeting the professor's team with Tim, Len and Mark discussed how the Robotic Humanoids AI influence was beginning to impinge on the human, social and business environment and it was decided to put the question to 'Quanto' the Professor's humanoid assistant who had been well versed and trained in the application of AI.

James walked over to the window where 'Quanto' was taking in the sun and daylight and said.

"Quanto, wake up."

"Yes, my Master."

"How will AI applications influence our living and working lives?"

'Quanto' answers emphatically.

"It is important that humans realise and learns that their understanding of Artificial Intelligence is beyond the level of the highest IQ Quotient of the human brain and so you must use and rely on the application of the Quantum Field, but you will not be dealing with something ultra- small, but something ultra-big, infinite, and absolute. Which means you will be involved and dealing with every aspect of your future technical, social, educational and business environment within your human lives?"

They all remained quiet as the professor, slowly nodding his head said.

"So, there you have it, we need to study the physics of the Quantum Field and know how to use its infinite power to control our use of AI and overcome the Robotic Humanoids controlling all the aspects of our future lives."

* * *

Note: Robotic Humanoids book 3 to follow (May 2025) (AI siblings).

Working Title: The educational Humanoid and Human AI influence within our schools. (fiction)

www.evansteve.com[1]

evans.steve@yahoo.co.uk

---

1. https://www.evansteve.com/

Don't miss out!

Visit the website below and you can sign up to receive emails whenever Steve Evans publishes a new book. There's no charge and no obligation.

https://books2read.com/r/B-A-NVWU-JLUFF

BOOKS 2 READ

Connecting independent readers to independent writers.

Did you love *Robotic Humamoids Book 2.*? Then you should read *Robotic Humanoids.*[2] by Steve Earle!

In this novella of 100 pages we tell the story of how the production of an advanced robotic brain resulted in the formation of Robotic Humanoids which vertually took over the administration of the whole world and in order to maintain their continued robotic existance decided to clean up the worlds climatic and industrial pollution.

And in a UK London science lab, a young neurologist Jamie together with his two female assistants Anne and Mari were working on simulated Artificial Intelligence technology with a view to enable their developing synthetic model to simulate and synchronize the electronic vibrations of the human brain. With the help of their computer programmer colleague and their powerful digital computers

2. https://books2read.com/u/b6z2dy

3. https://books2read.com/u/b6z2dy

they worked out a digital circuit chip that appeared to accept and record the electronic vibrations from the synapsis activity of their brains.

With the creation of a basic structure of the human body the circuit boards and mechanical moving joints were covered and protected by a mesh to house the AI brain chip and supportive electronic circuits, a robotic human body framework was built to house the electronic network and bodily structure. The body was protected and covered in a synthetic gel of seaweed and silicon moldings which looked and acted like the flesh of a human body.

No nourishment or maintenance needed. It was the perfect robotic body totally operational from the intake of the solar energy from natural daylight and sun. With the implant of a humanoid brain chip that could function and coordinate the robotic limbs and make decisions by mentally using electronic vibrations and impulses of the synthetic human AI brain that appeared to be a million times more powerful than the human brain... and so the robotic Humanoids were created.

Also by Steve Evans

Robotic Humanoids.
Robotic Humamoids Book 2.

Watch for more at https://www.evansteve.com.

About the Author

Sales and Business Director. Now retired living in a small village in the New Forest, Southern England UK. Enjoy long walks observing nature, sitting in favourites spots dictating my writing notes as they occur in my fertile (I nearly said futile) imagination. Writing short stories, eBooks .. As a mature student at Manchester University studied creative writing and philosophy. Also in later years, (in retirement) completed a three-year playwriting course at Southampton University.Sales and Business Director. Now retired living in a small village in the New Forest, Southern England UK.

Read more at https://www.evansteve.com.

9 798822 726810